Dear Parent:

Psst . . . you're looking at the Super Secret Weapon of Reading. It's called comics.

STEP INTO READING® COMIC READERS are a perfect step in learning to read. They provide visual cues to the meaning of words and helpfully break out short pieces of dialogue into speech balloons.

Here are some terms commonly associated with comics:

PANEL: A section of a comic with a box drawn around it.
CAPTION: Narration that helps set the scene.
SPEECH BALLOON: A bubble containing dialogue.
GUTTER: The space between panels.

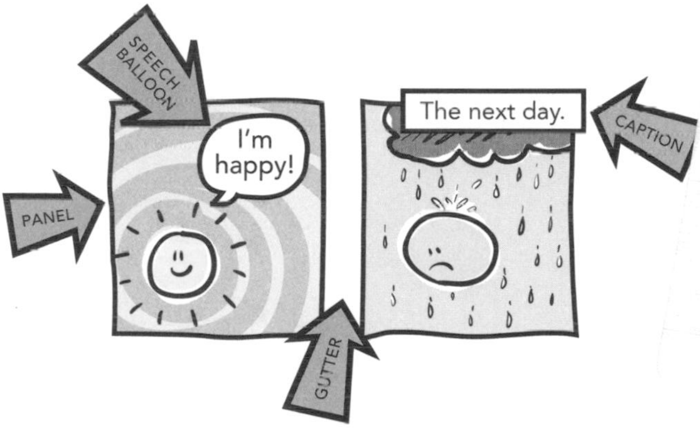

SPEECH BALLOON
PANEL
I'm happy!
The next day.
CAPTION
GUTTER

Tips for reading comics with your child:

- **Have your child read the speech balloons while you read the captions.**
- **Ask your child: What is a character feeling? How can you tell?**
- **Have your child draw a comic showing what happens after the book is finished.**

STEP INTO READING® COMIC READERS are designed to engage and to provide an empowering reading experience. They are also fun. The best-kept secret of comics is that they create lifelong readers. **And that will make you the real hero of the story!**

Jennifer L. Holm and Matthew Holm
Co-creators of the Babymouse and Squish series

For Megan, who lent me her pencil —D.M.R.

*To my wife, Jeong Eun, and my son, Hale,
who give me unconditional support and love
—W.J.J.*

Text copyright © 2013 by Dana Meachen Rau
Cover art and interior illustrations copyright © 2013 by Wook Jin Jung

Visit us on the Web!
StepIntoReading.com
randomhouse.com/kids

Educators and librarians, for a variety of teaching tools, visit us at
randomhouse.com/teachers

Library of Congress Cataloging-in-Publication Data
Rau, Dana Meachen
Robot, go Bot! / by Dana Meachen Rau ; illustrated by Wook Jin Jung.
    p. cm.
"A Step 1 Comic Reader."
Summary: A young girl makes so many demands on the robot she has constructed that he runs away.
ISBN 978-0-375-87083-5 (trade pbk.) — ISBN 978-0-375-97083-2 (lib. bdg.) —
ISBN 978-0-375-98101-2 (ebook) — ISBN 978-0-449-81429-1 (read & listen ebook)
[1. Robots—Fiction. 2. Robots—Cartoons and comics. 3. Cartoons and comics.]
I. Jung, Wook Jin, ill. II. Title.
PZ8.3.R232Go 2013   [E]—dc23   2012027691

Printed in the United States of America
10 9 8 7 6 5 4 3 2 1

STEP INTO READING®

STEP 1

Robot, Go Bot!

A COMIC READER

by Dana Meachen Rau

illustrated by Wook Jin Jung

Random House 🏠 New York

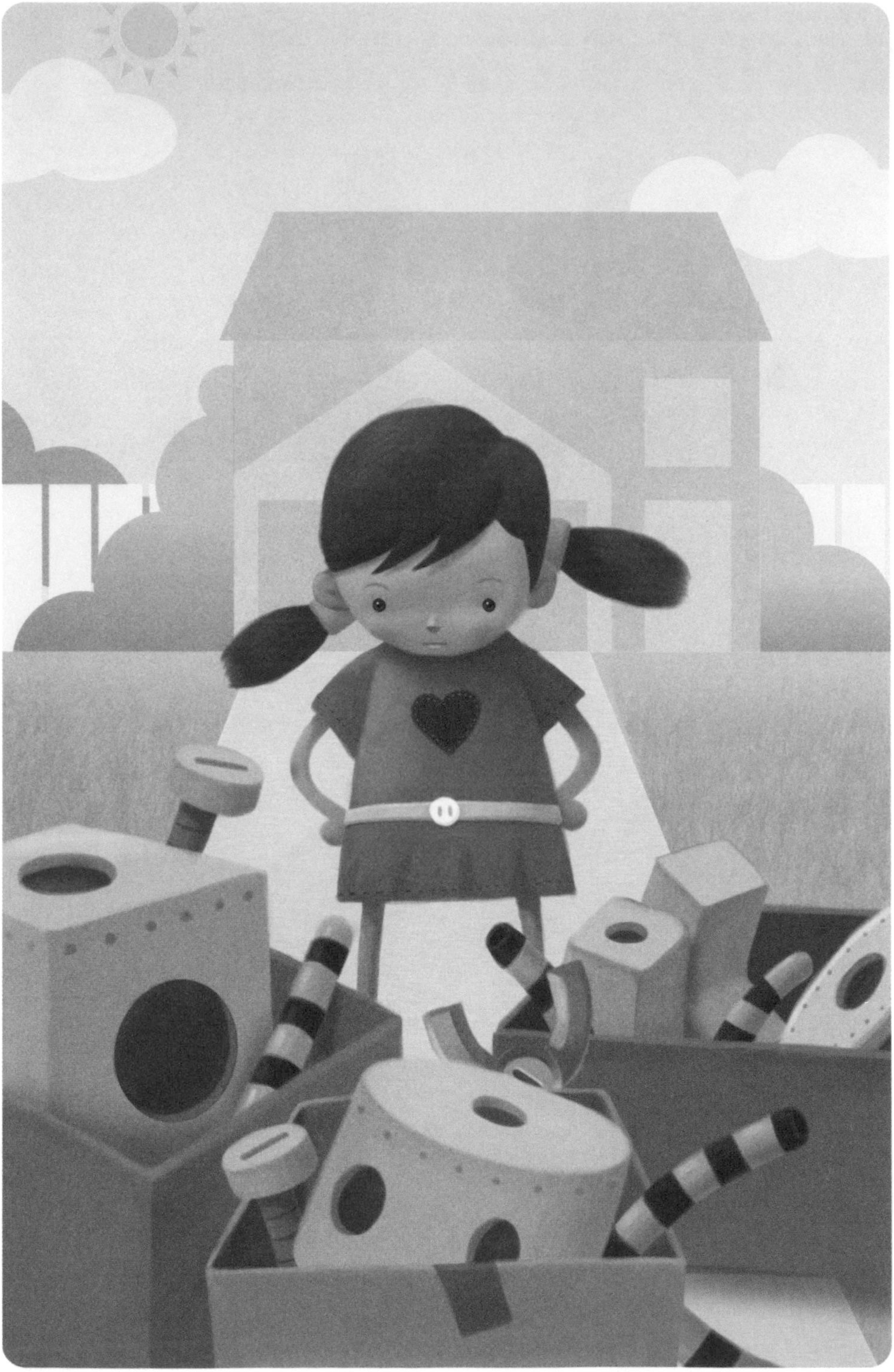

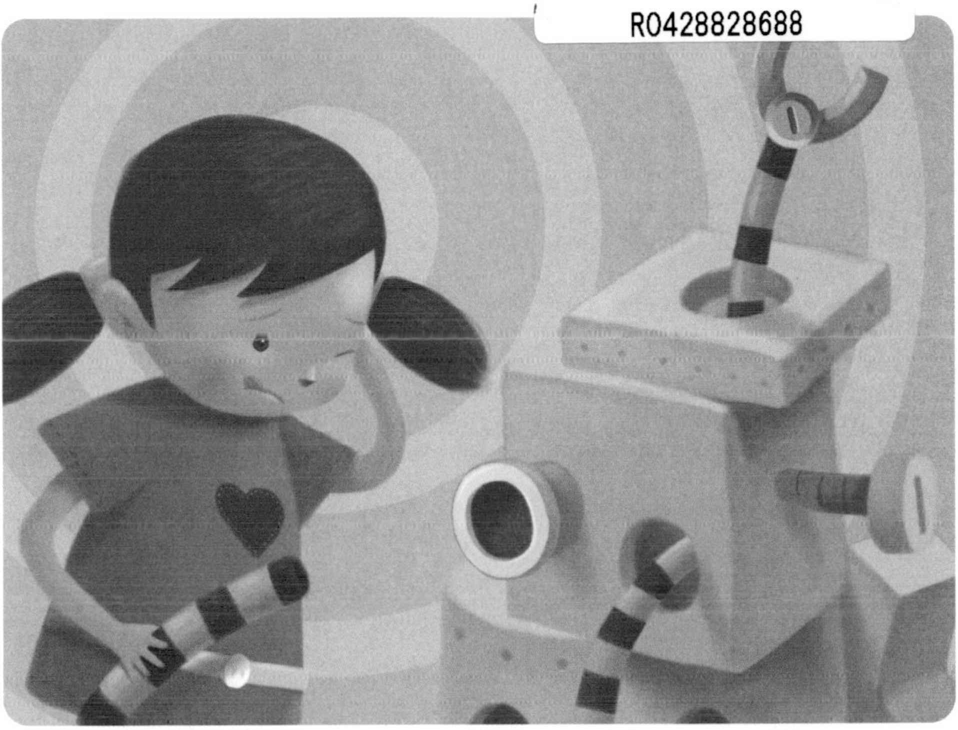

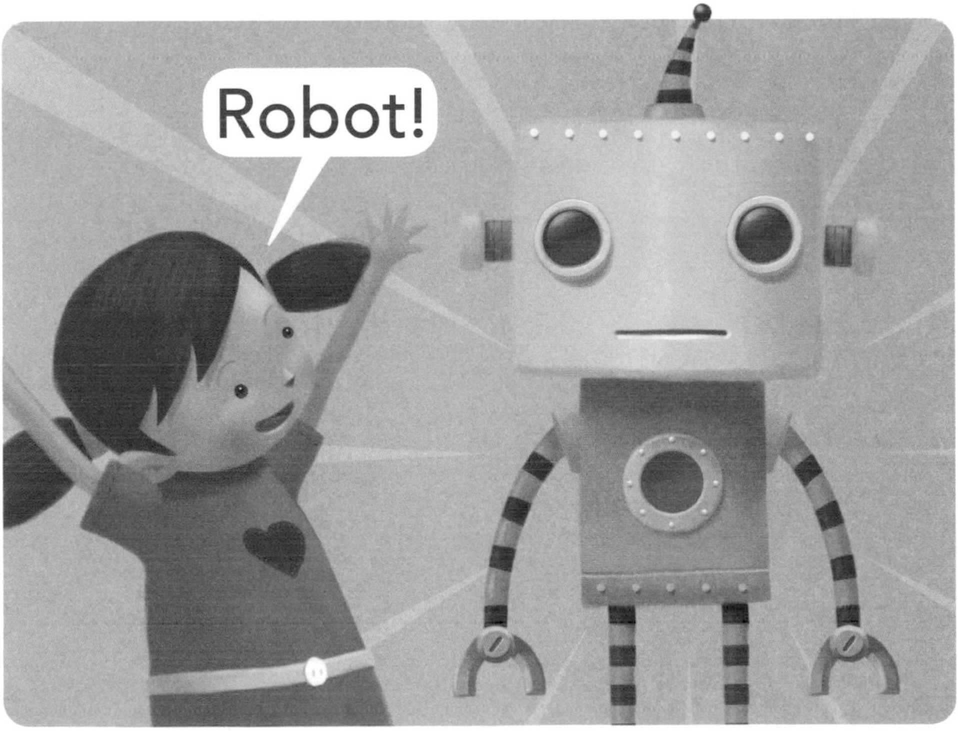
Robot!

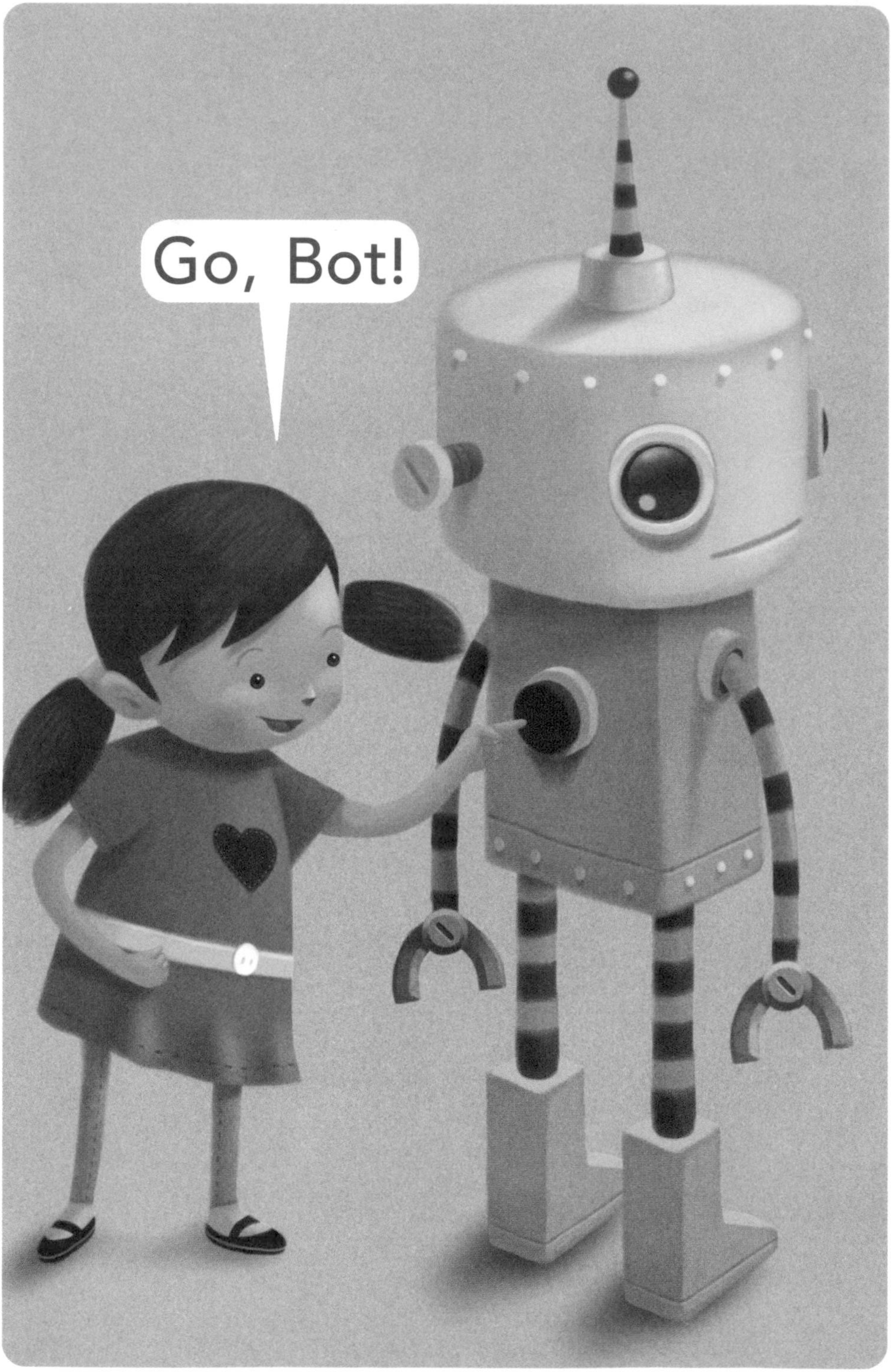
Go, Bot!

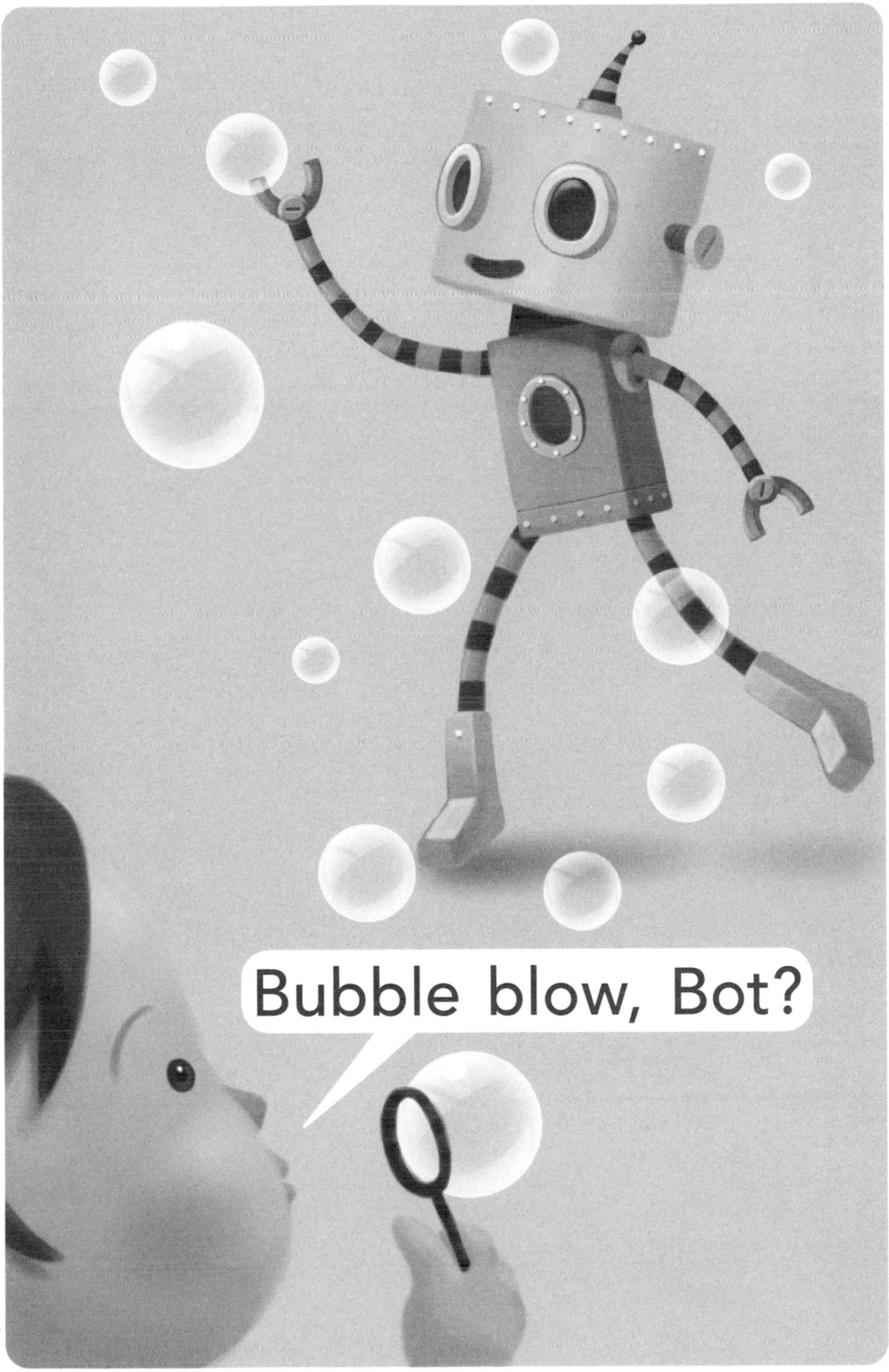
Bubble blow, Bot?

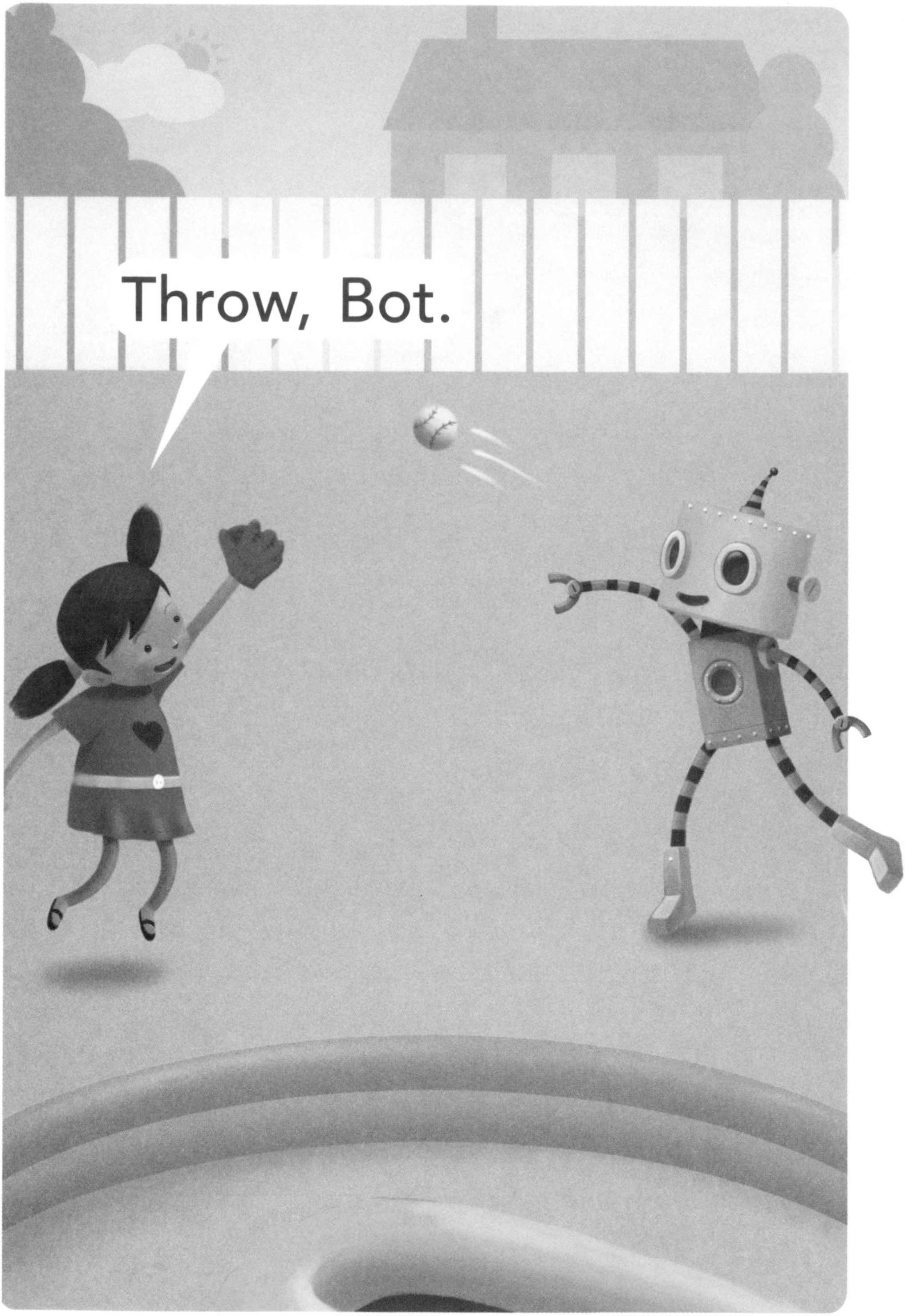
Throw, Bot.

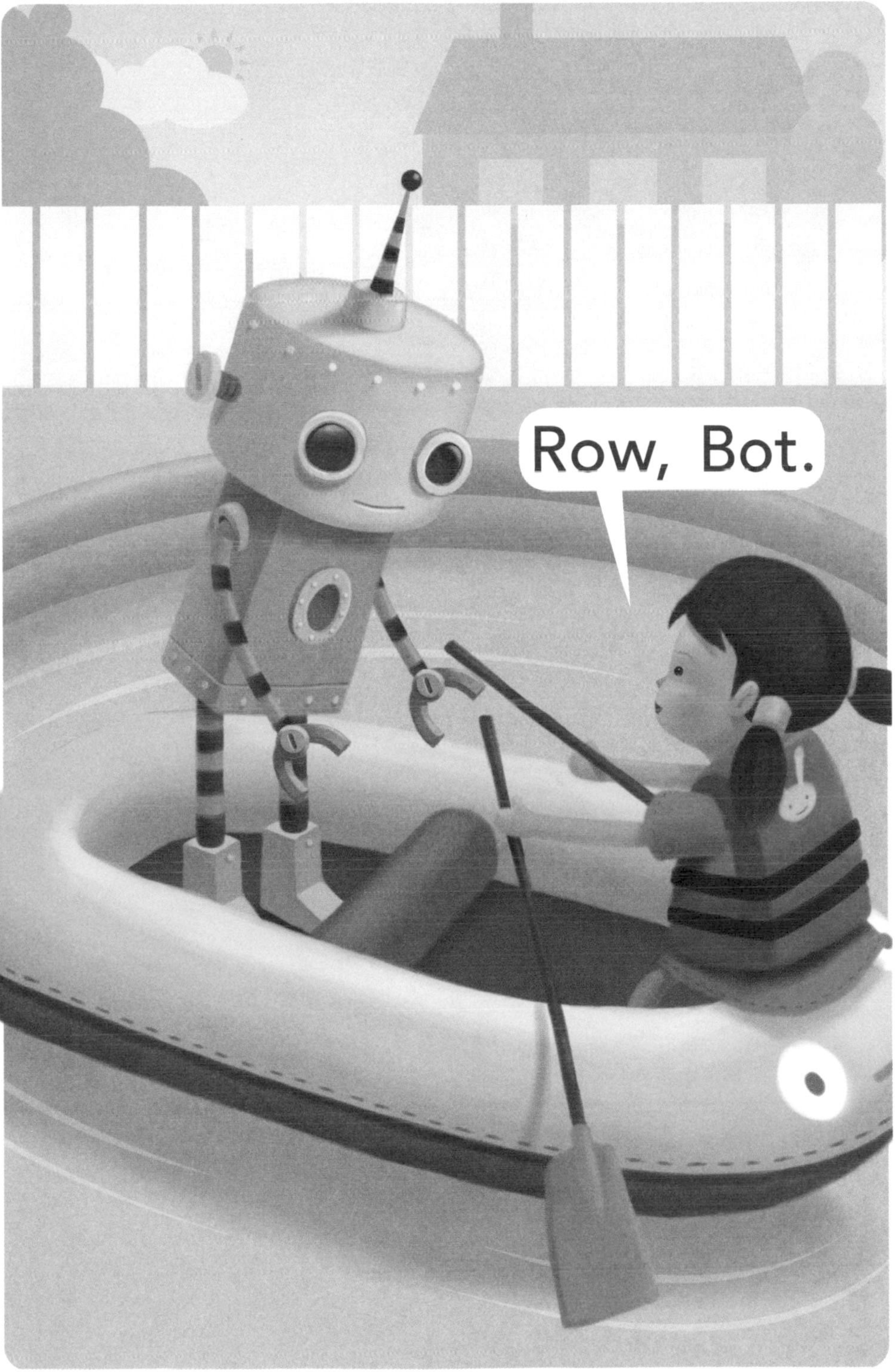
Row, Bot.

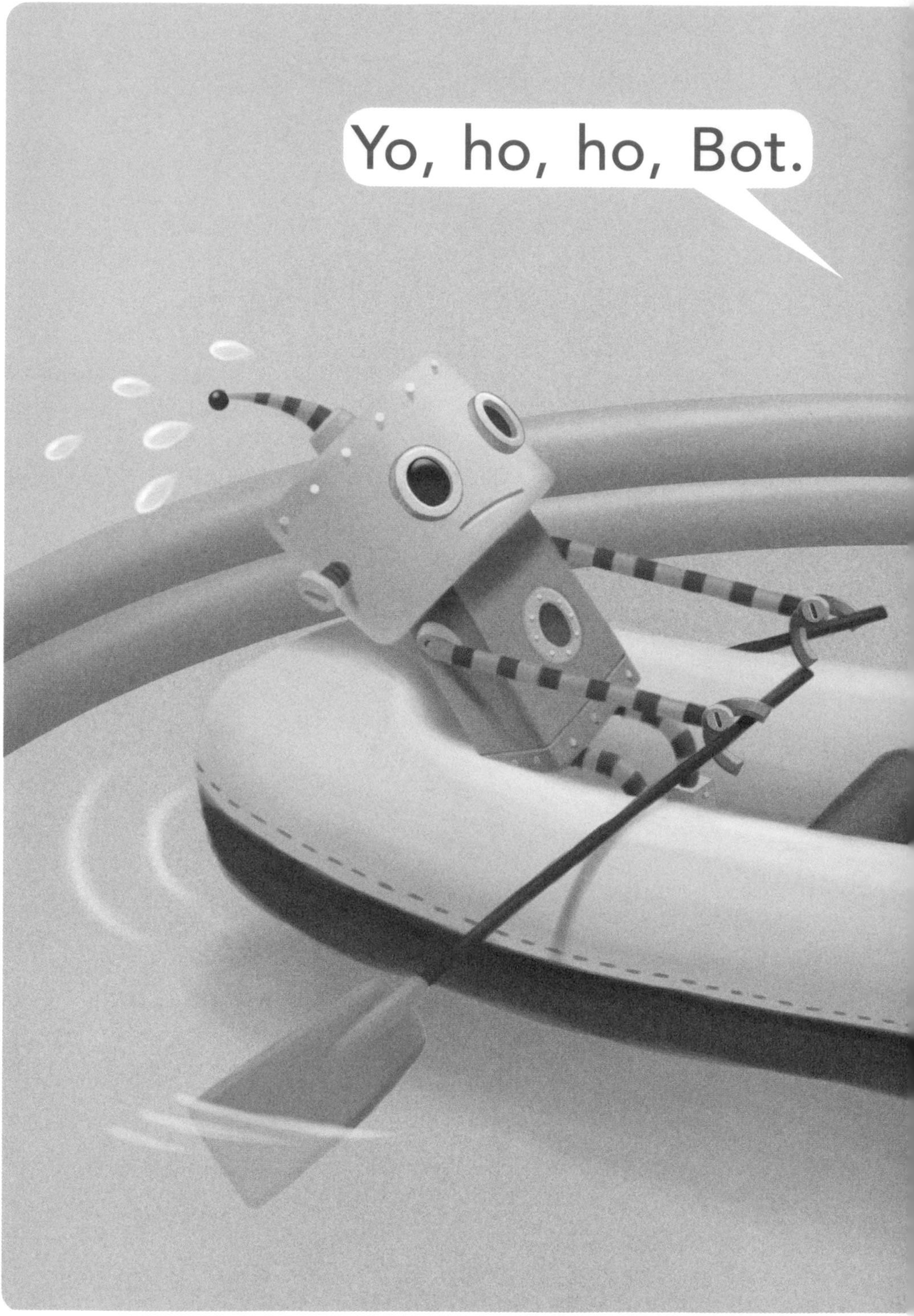
Yo, ho, ho, Bot.

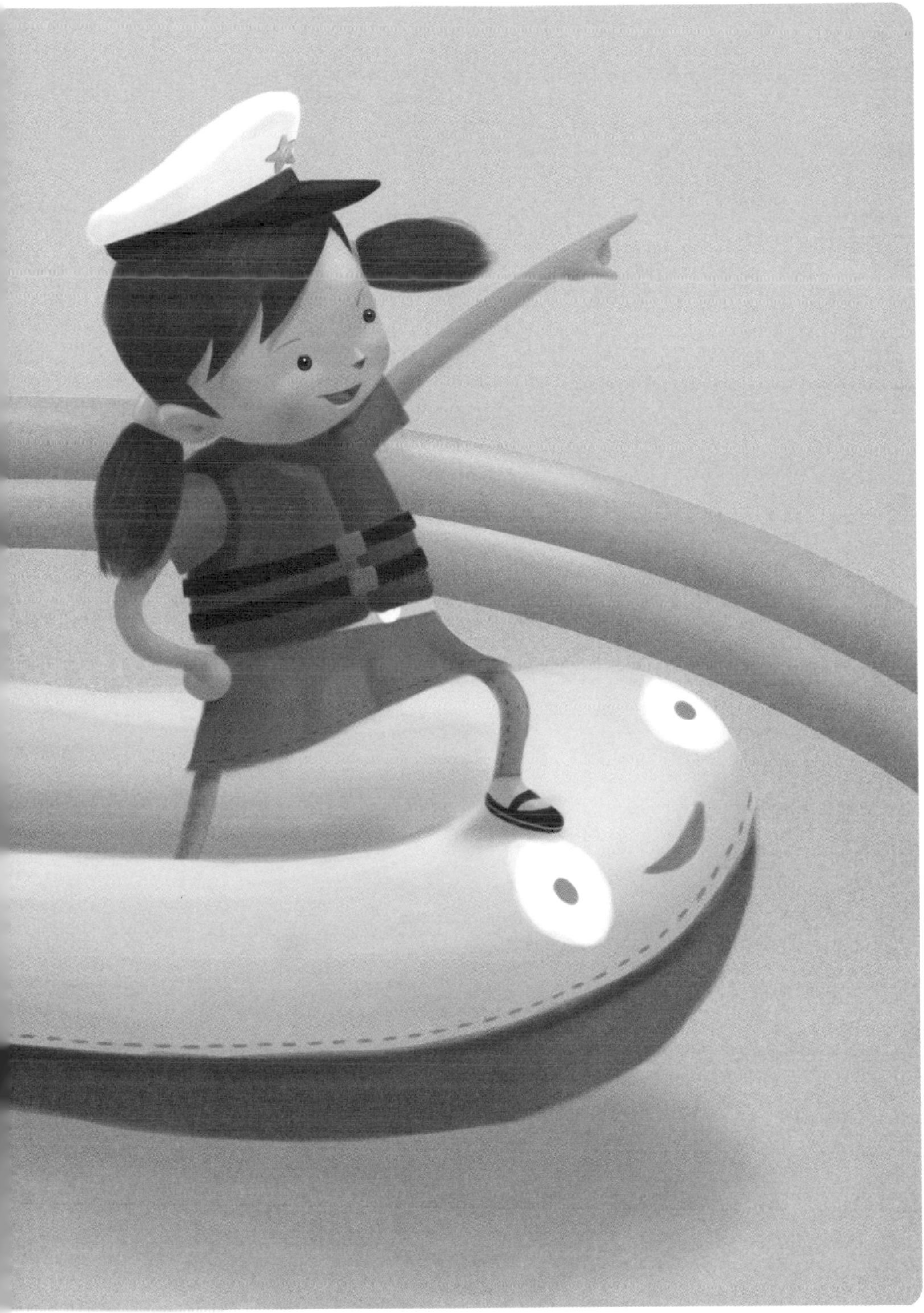

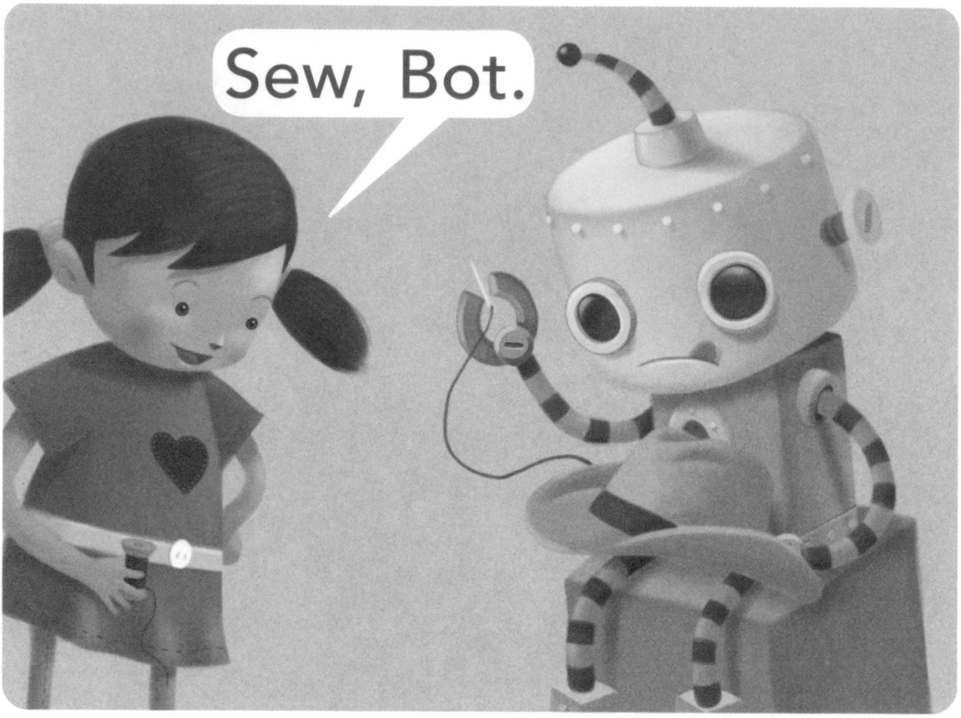
Sew, Bot.

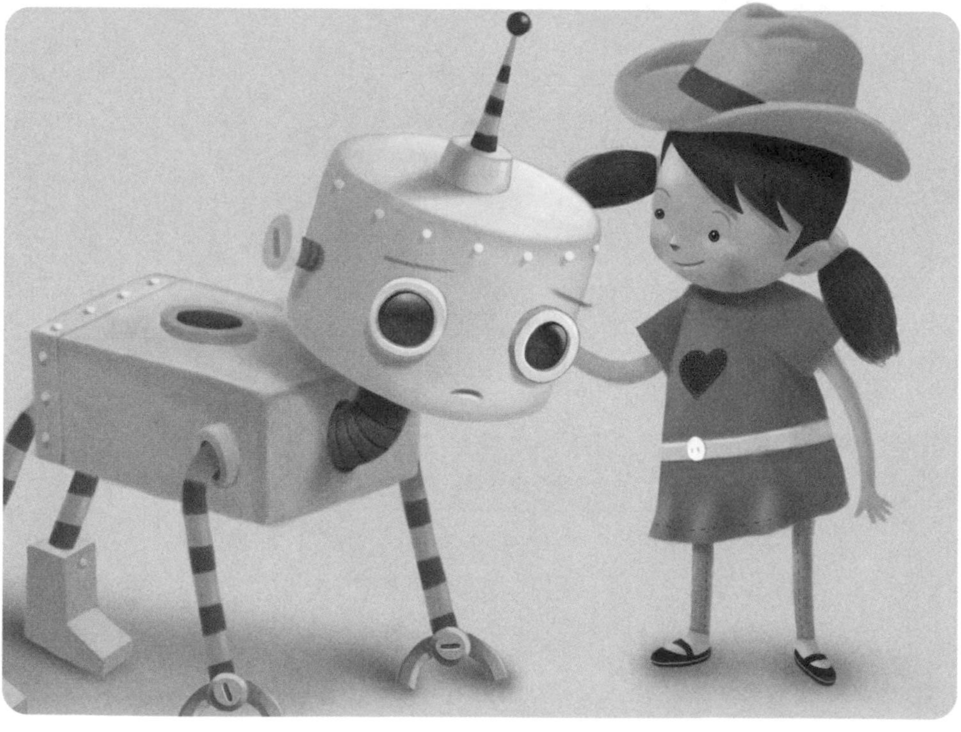

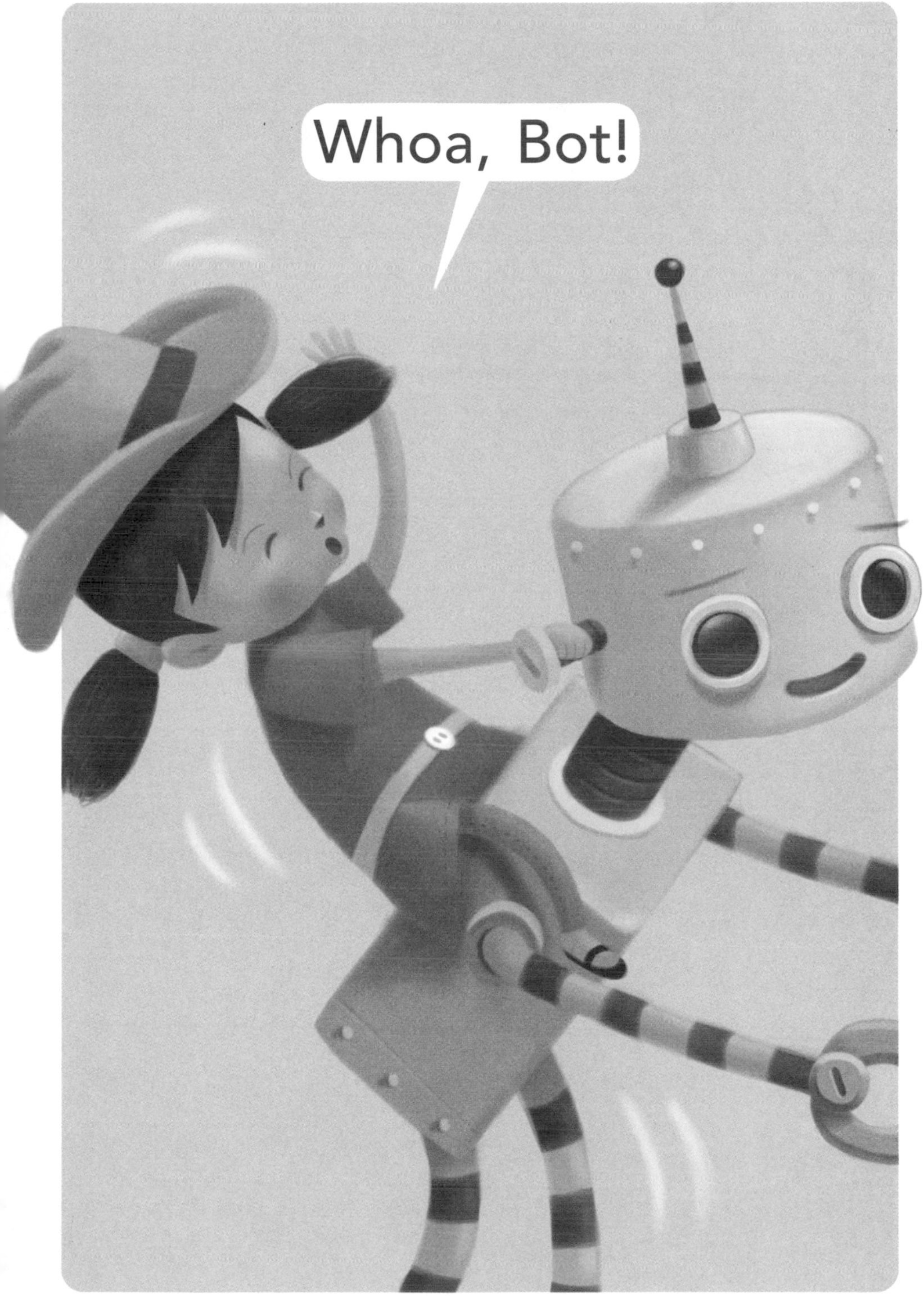
Whoa, Bot!

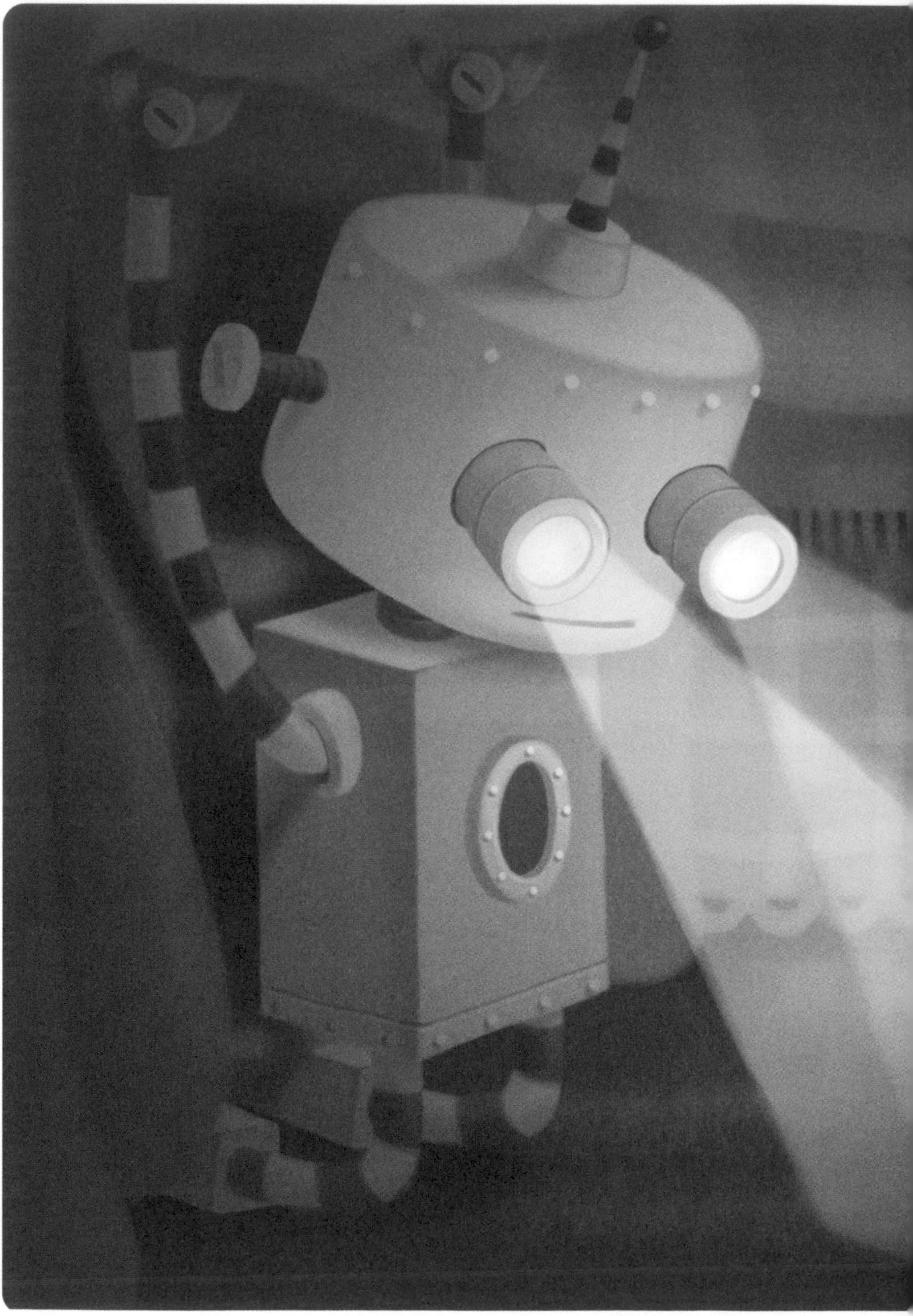

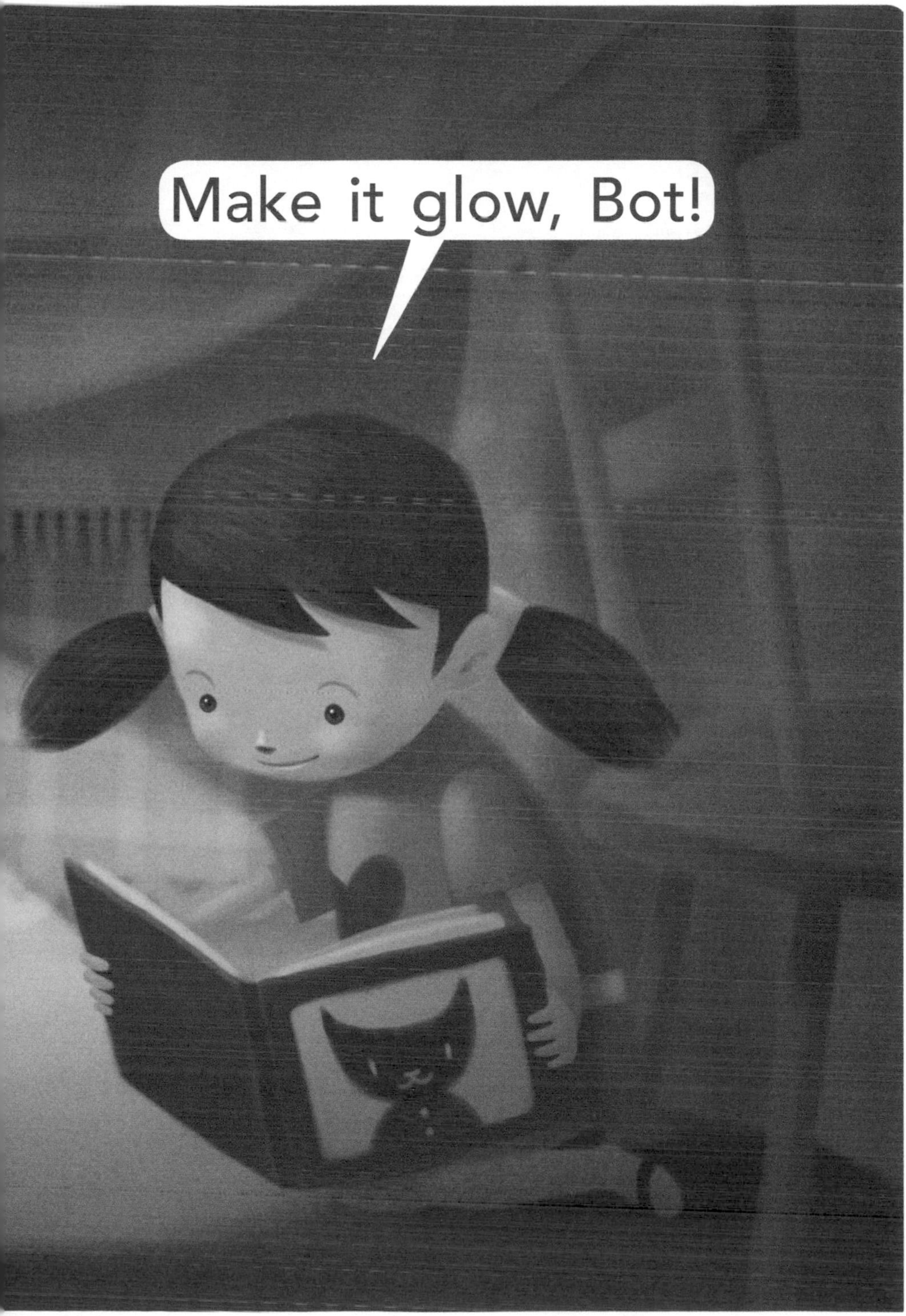
Make it glow, Bot!

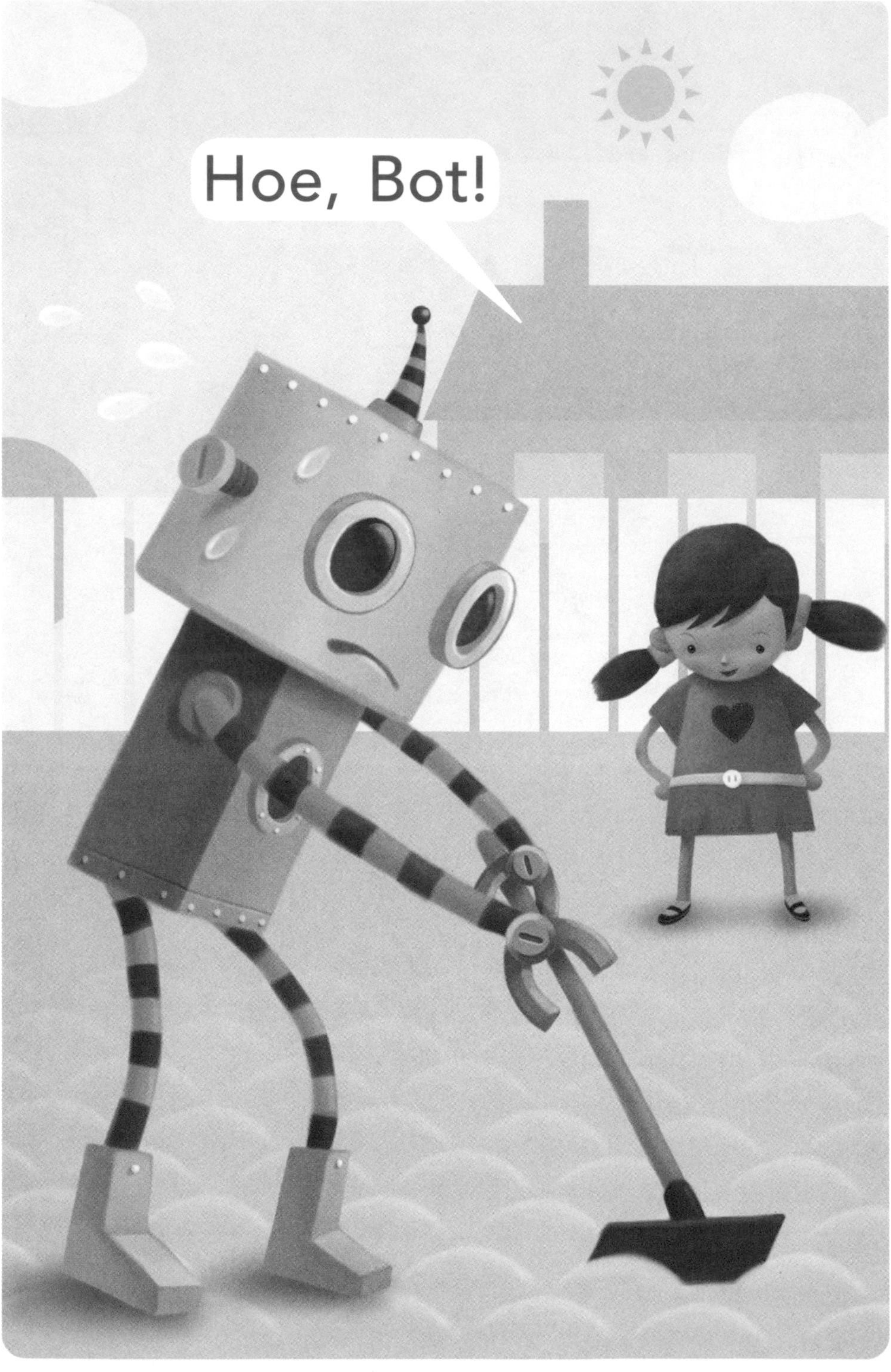
Hoe, Bot!

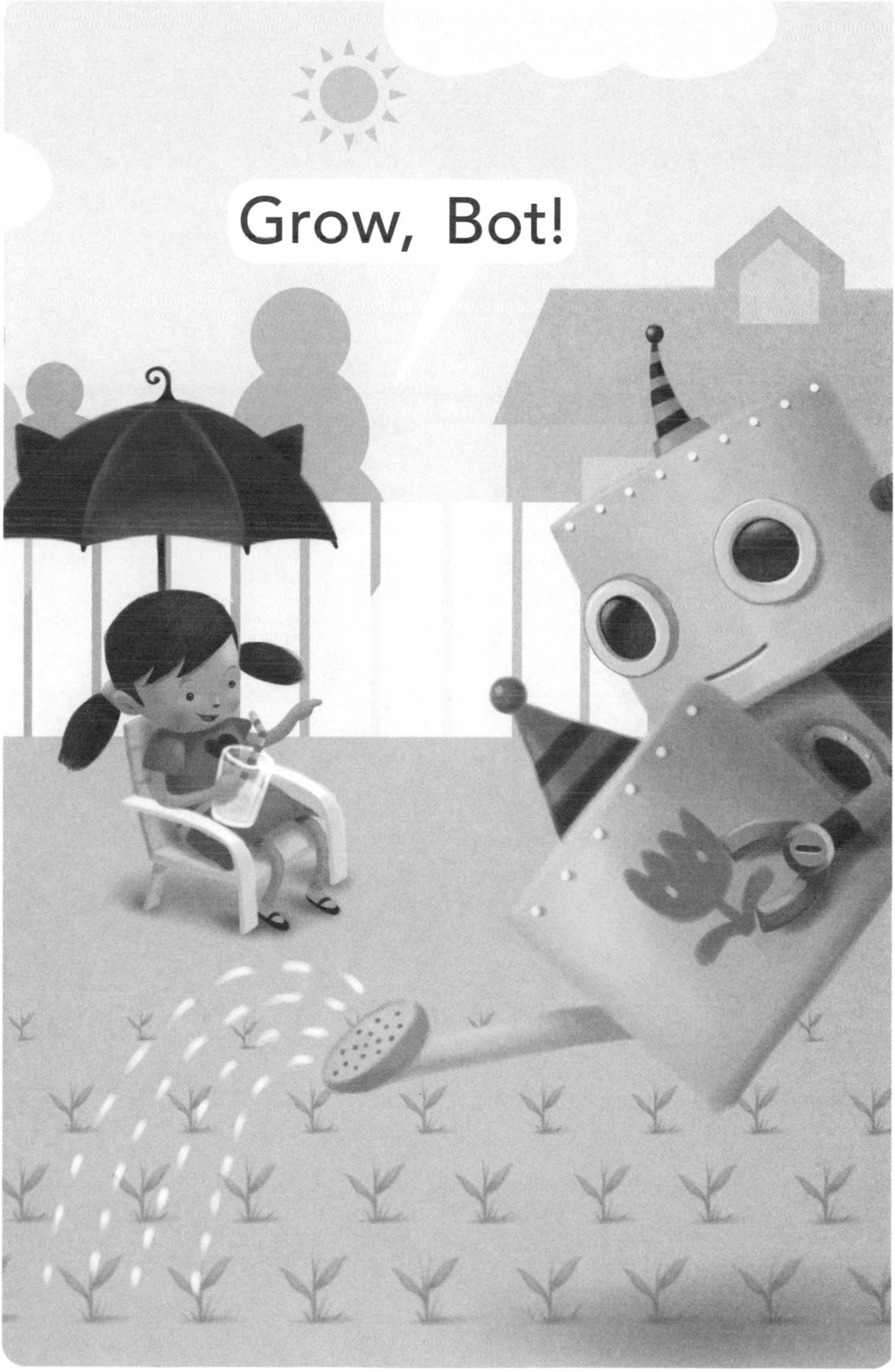
Grow, Bot!

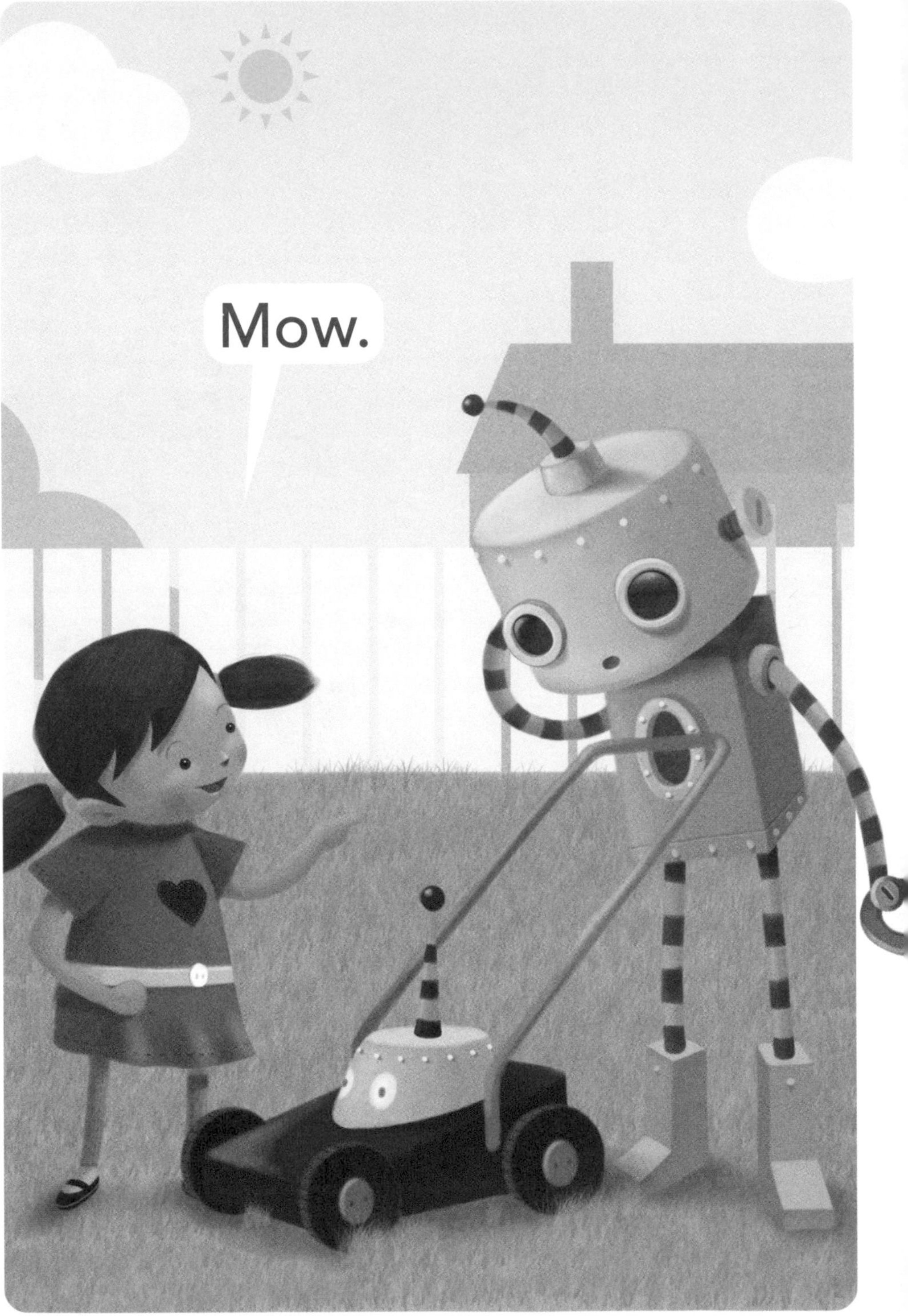
Mow.

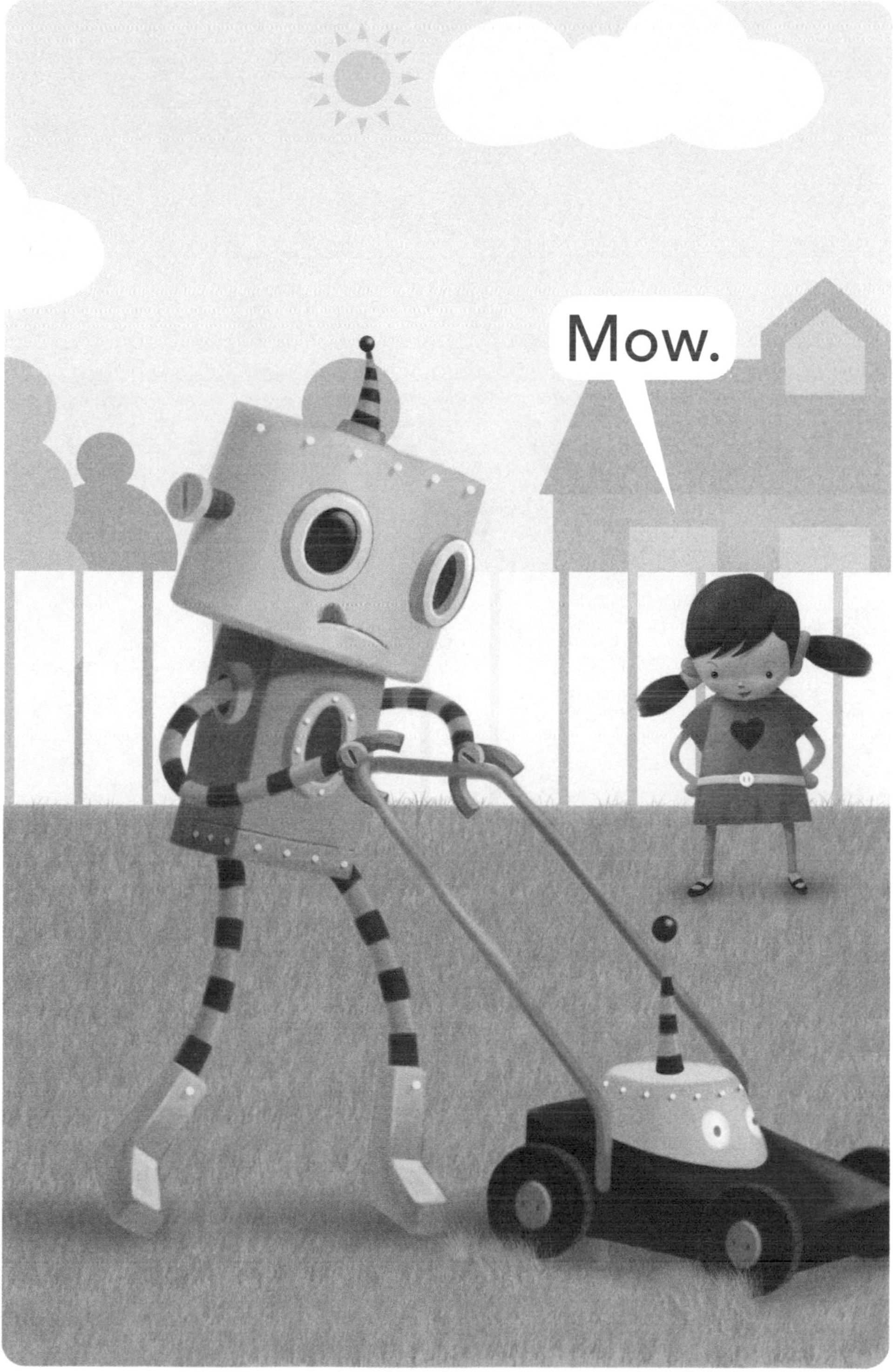
Mow.

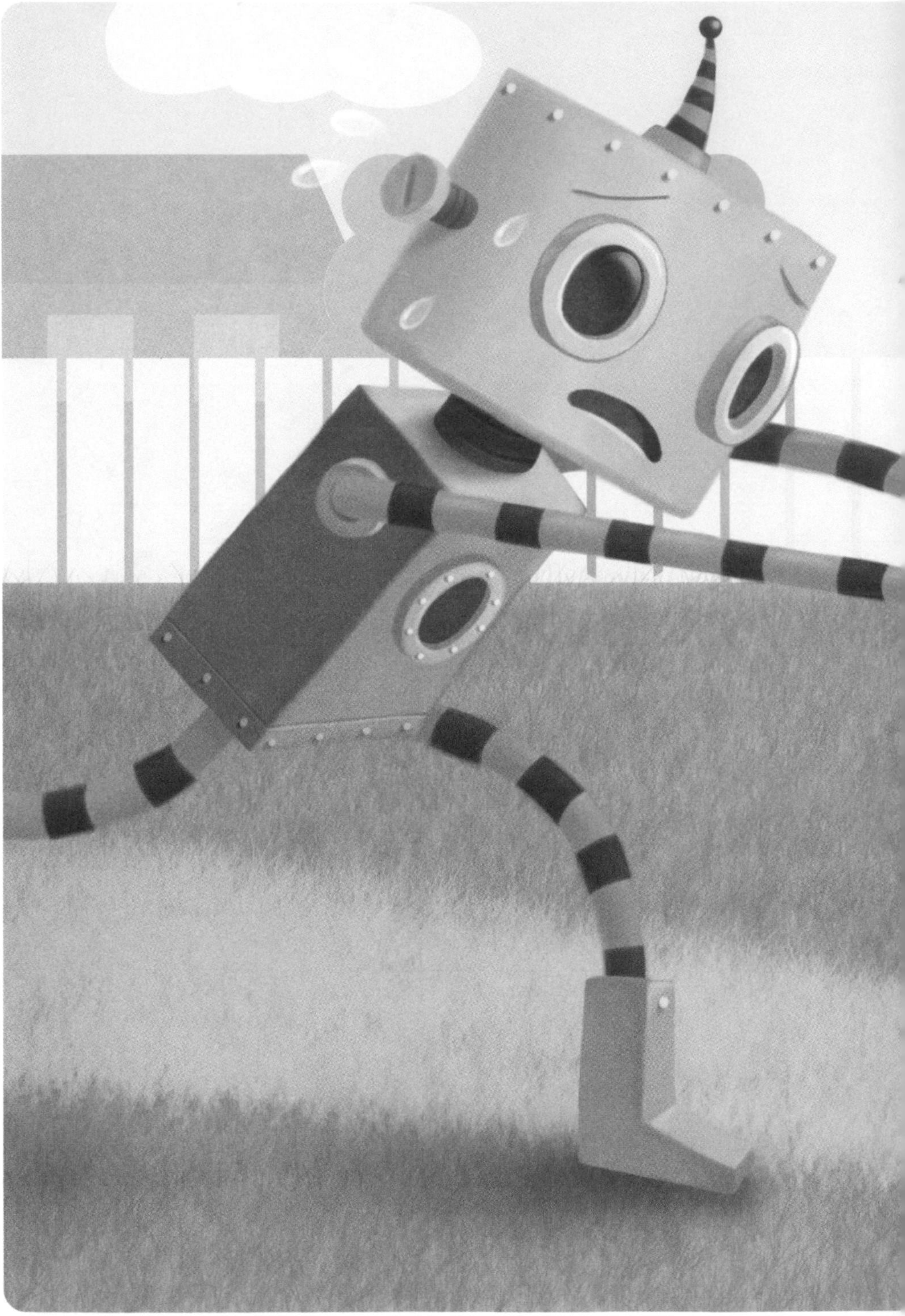

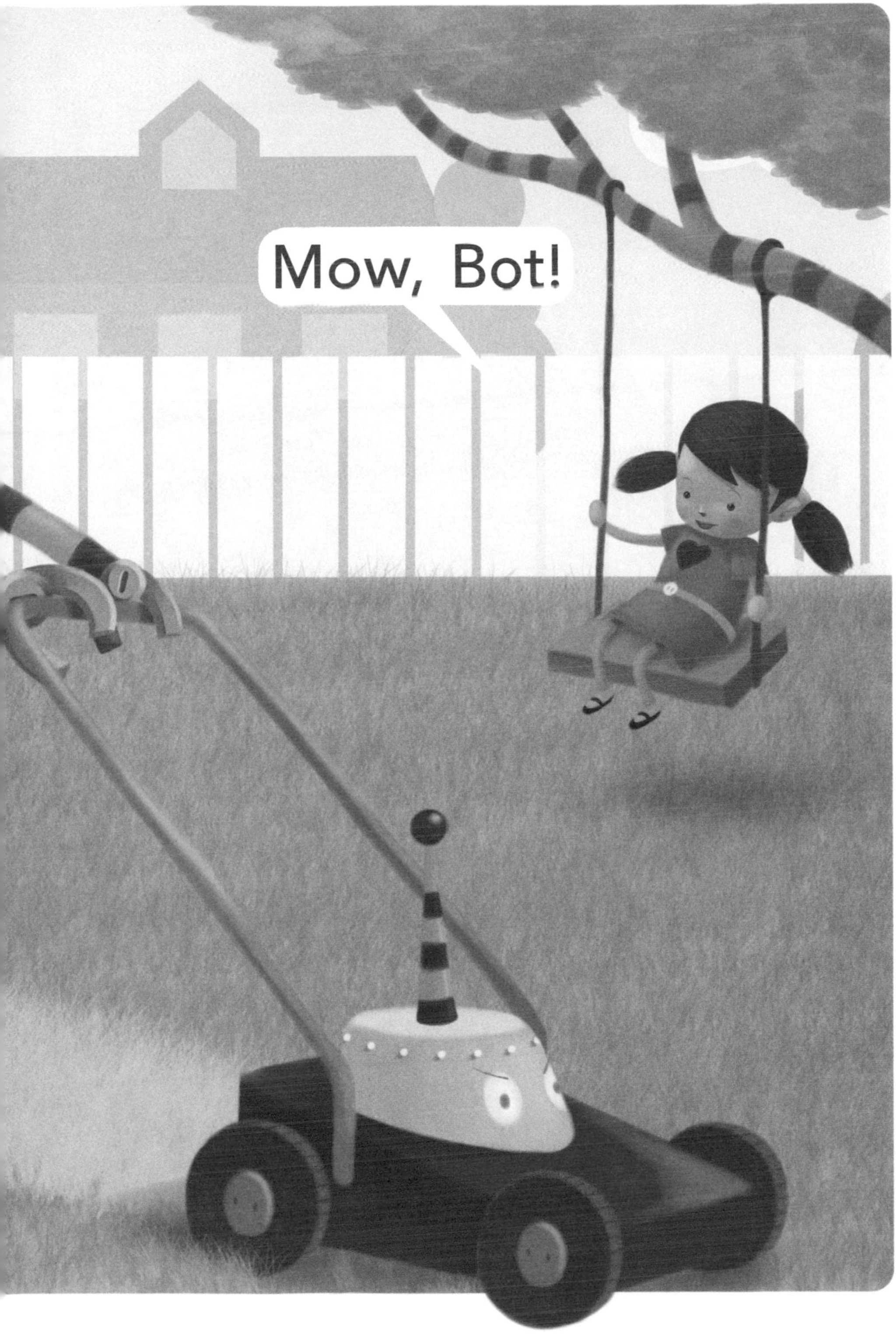
Mow, Bot!

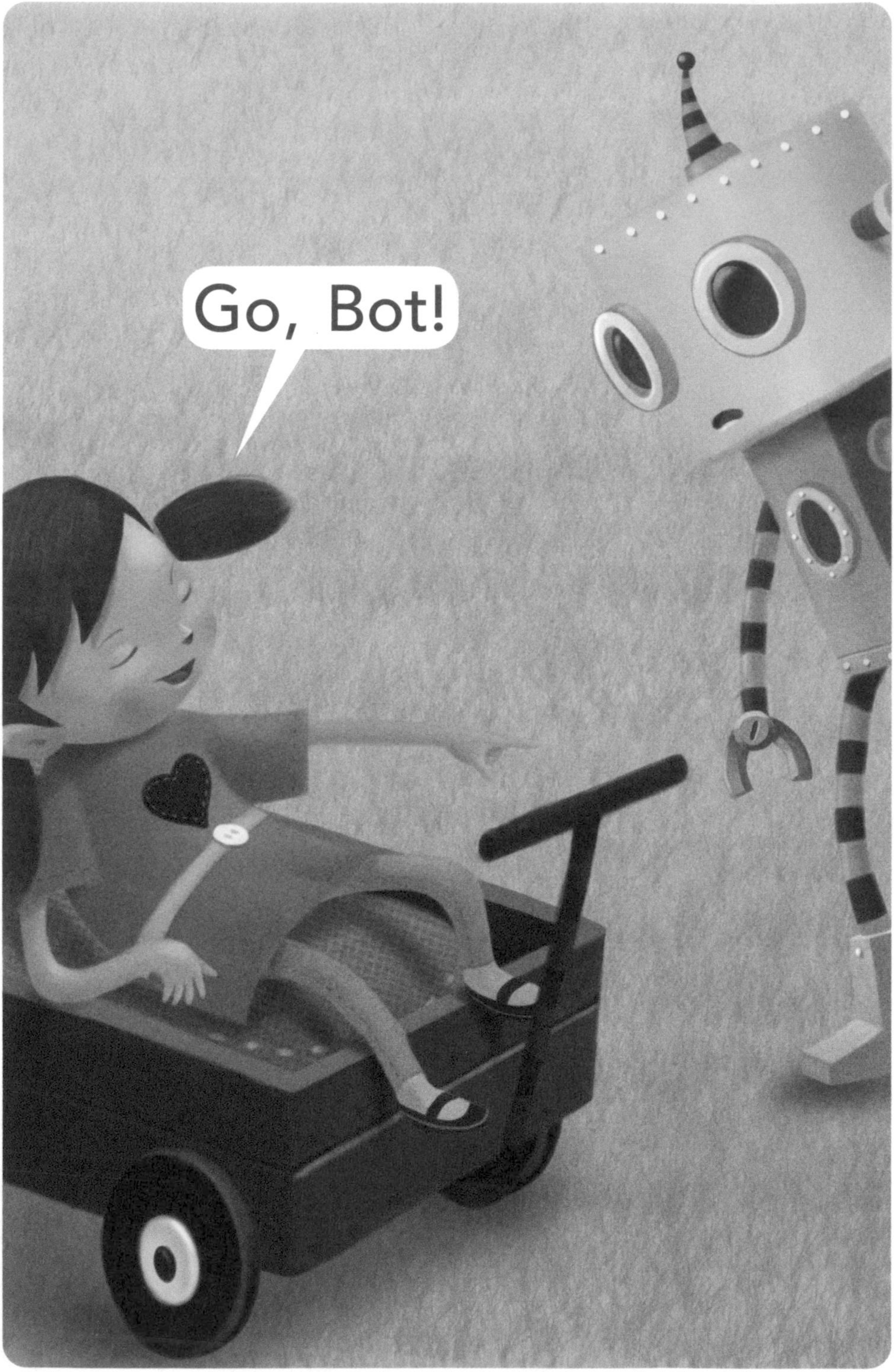
Go, Bot!

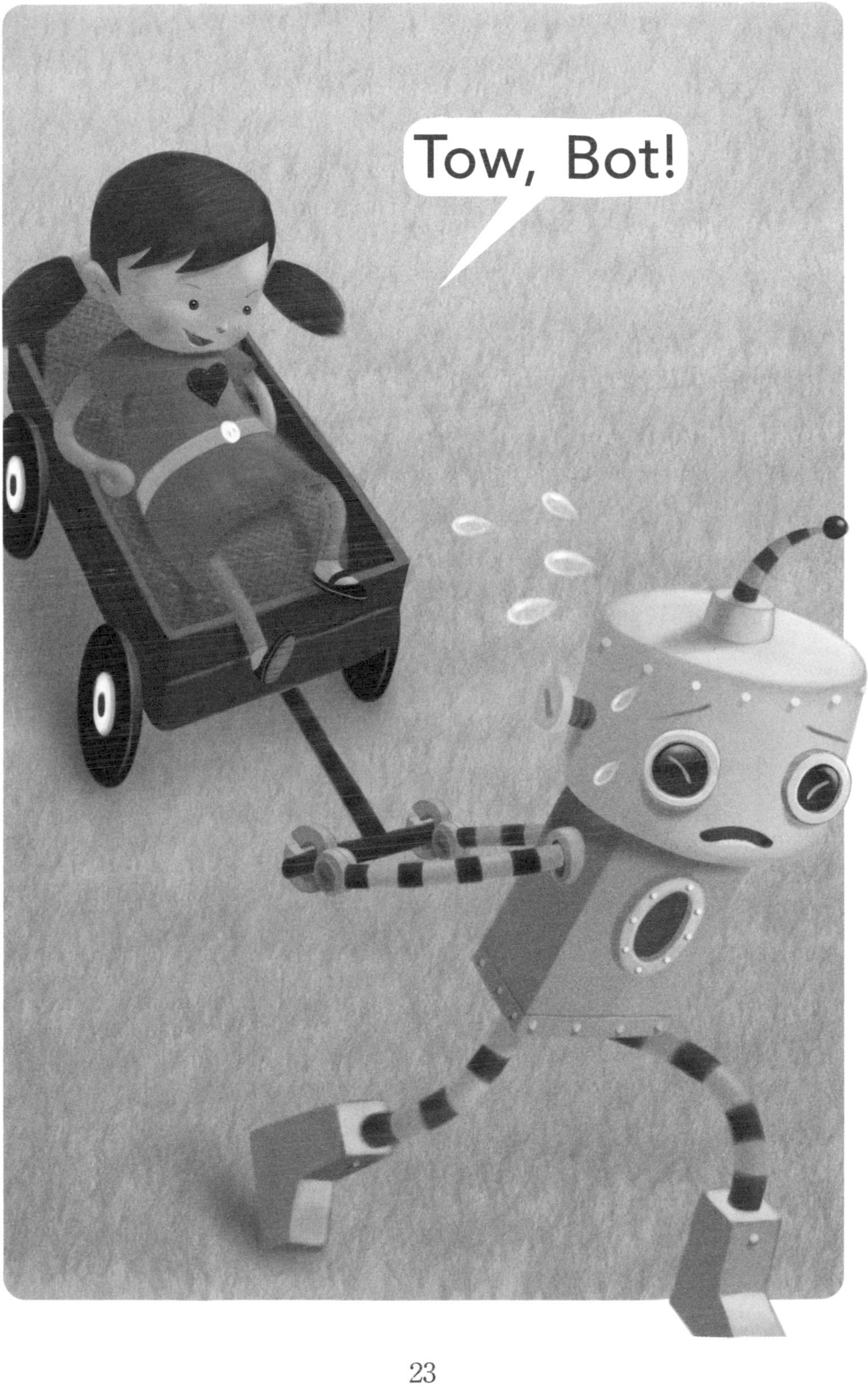
Tow, Bot!

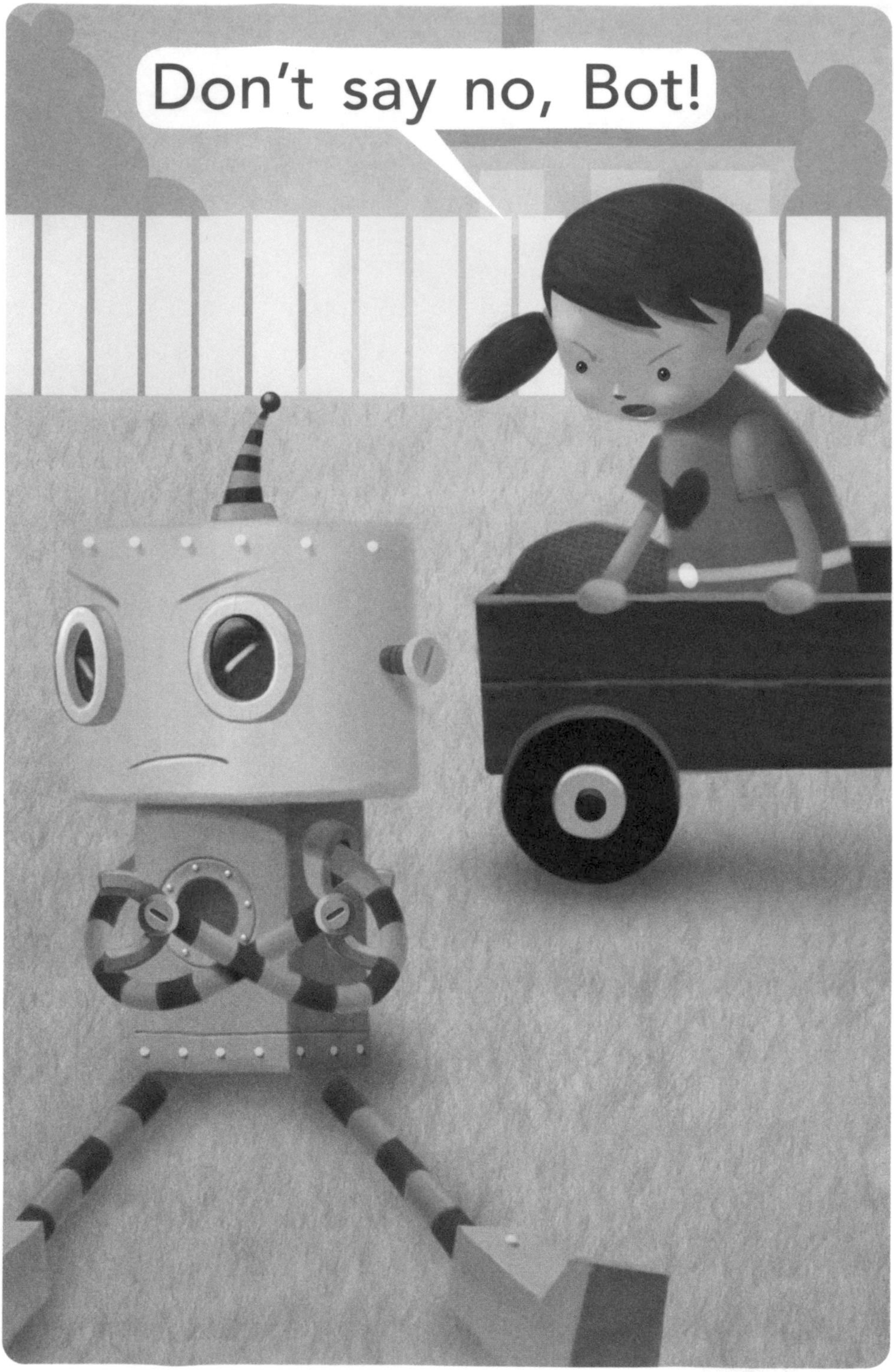
Don’t say no, Bot!

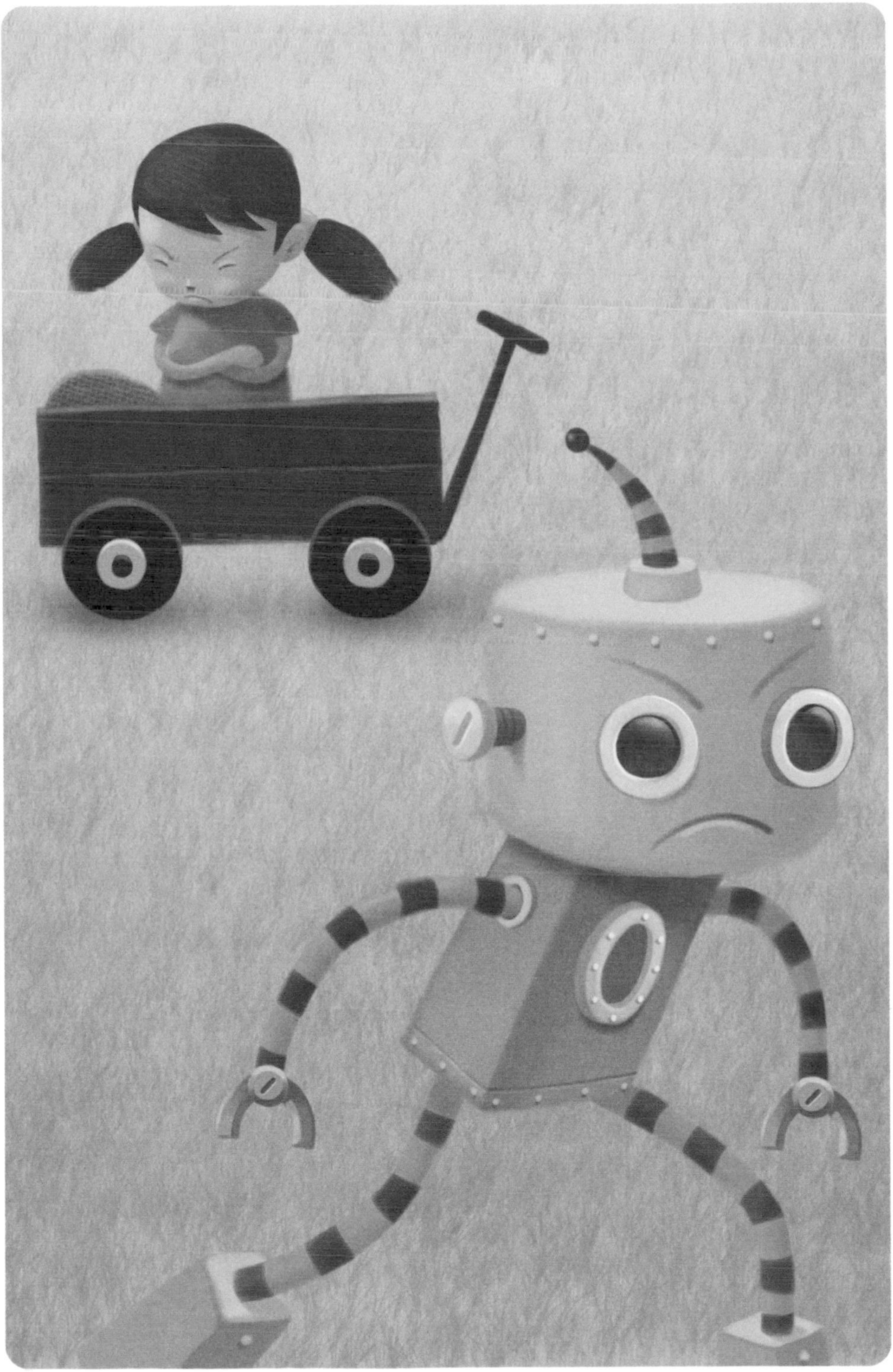

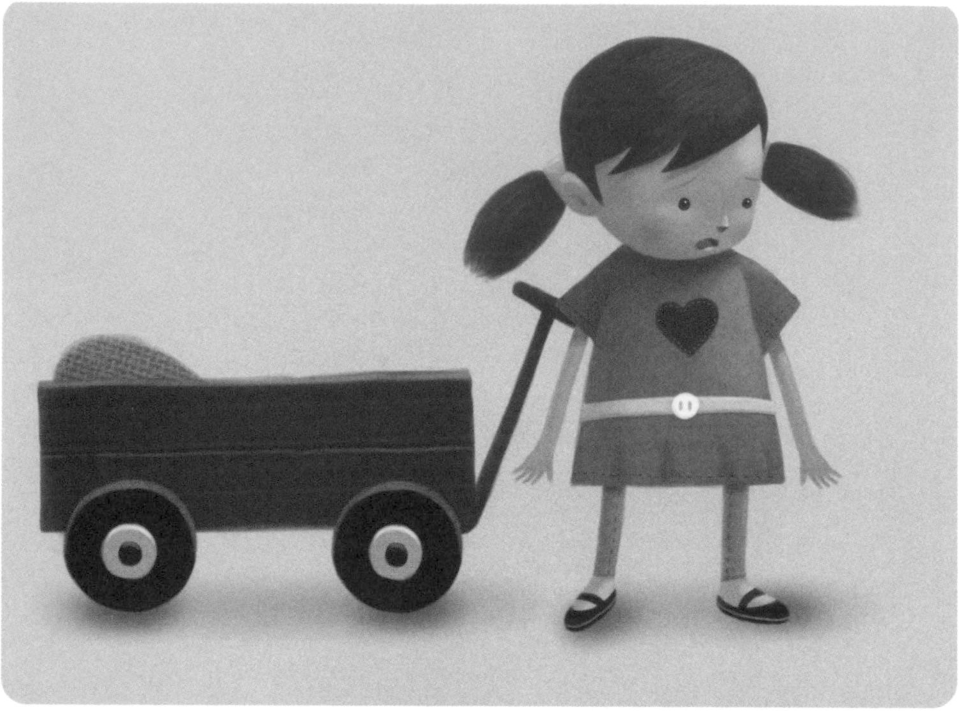

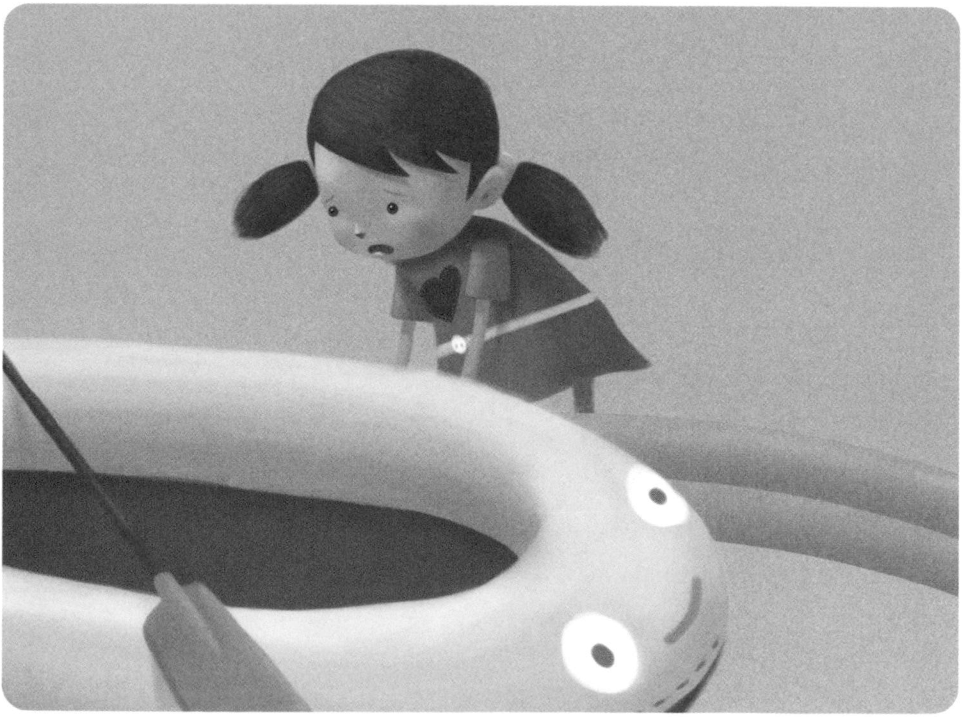

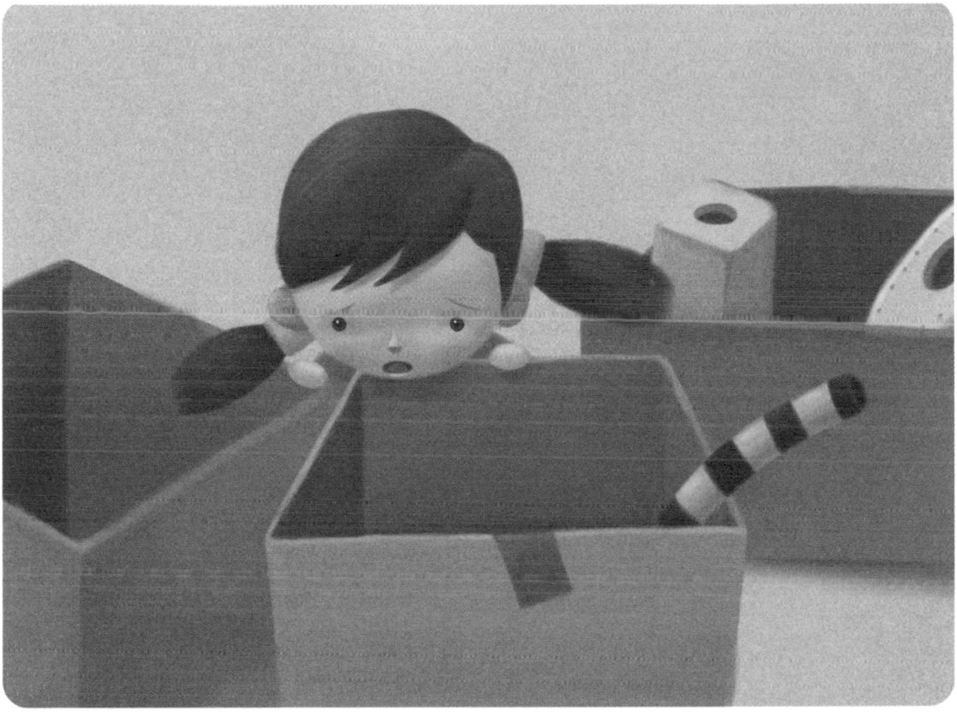

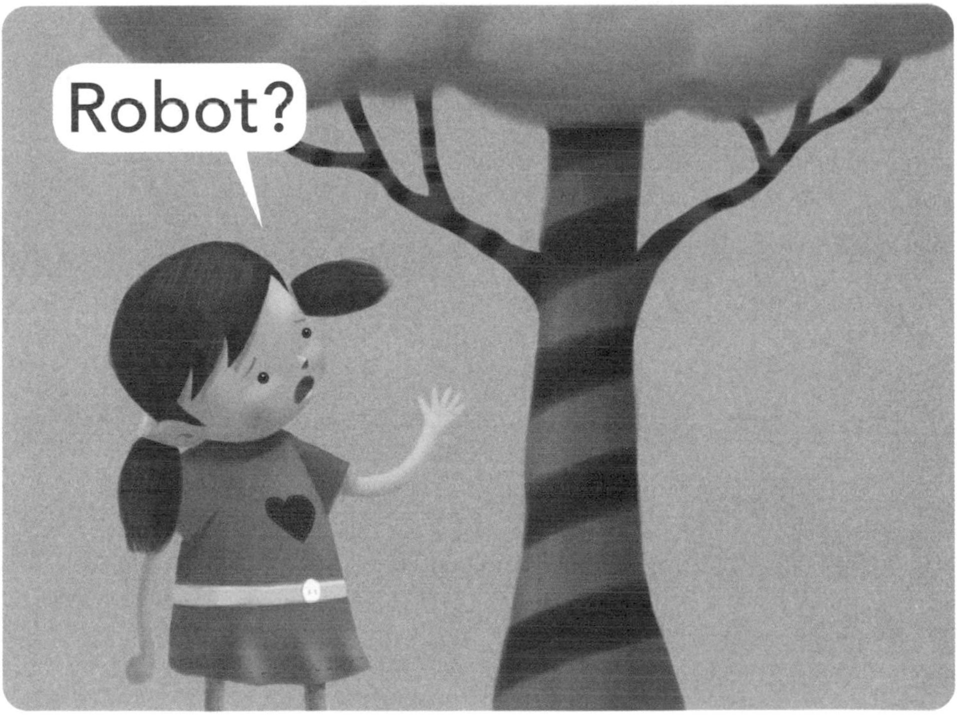
Robot?

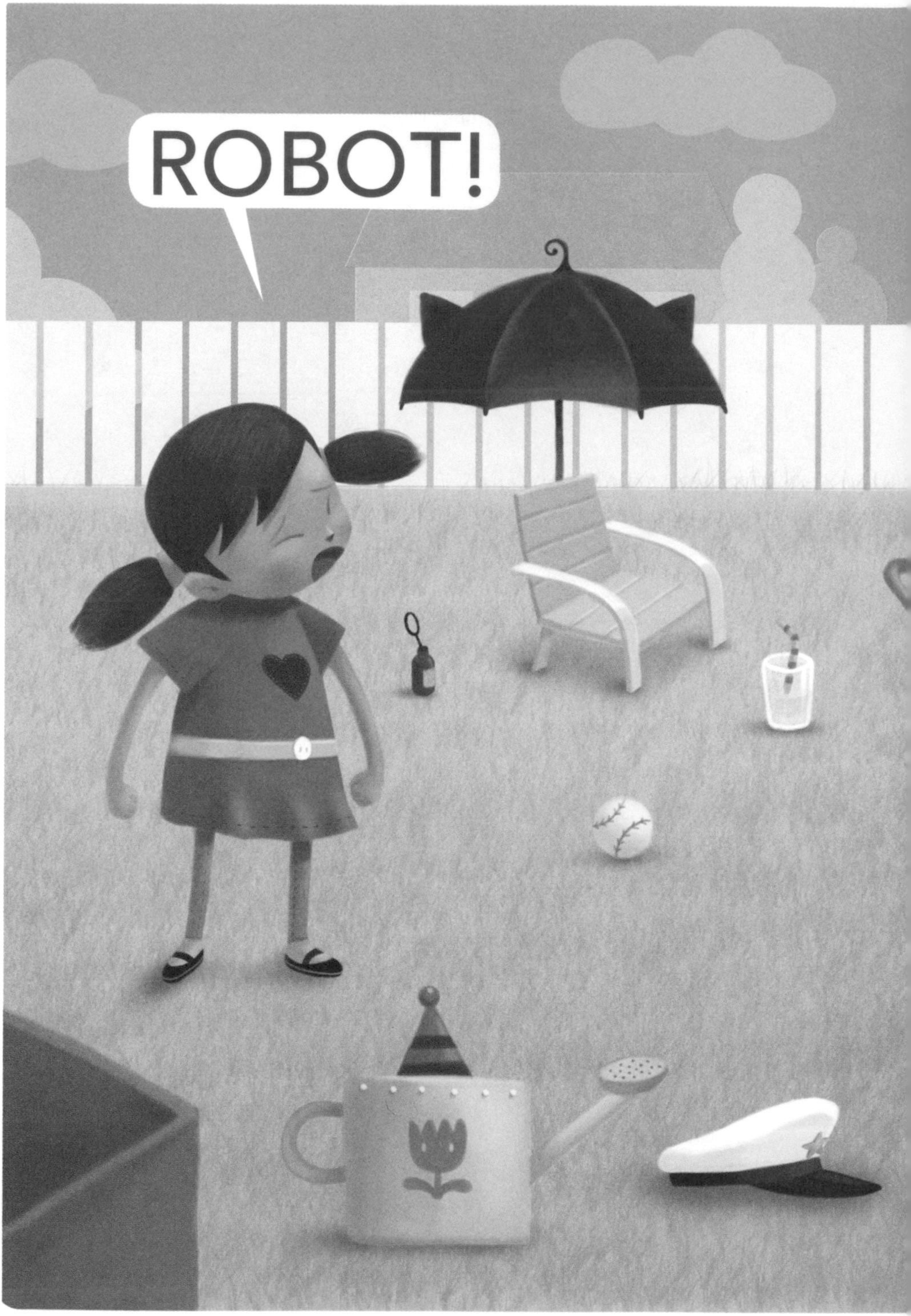
ROBOT!

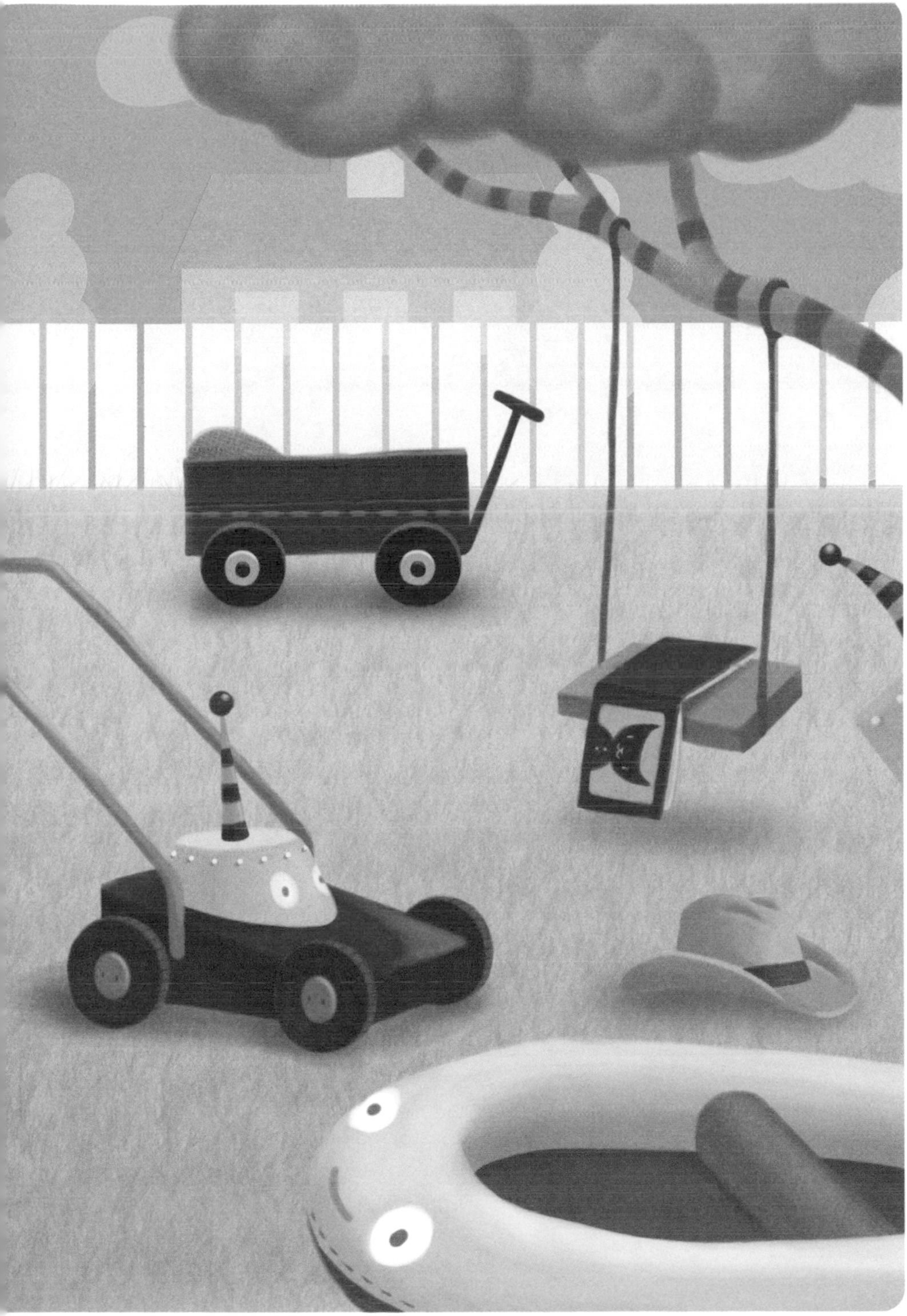

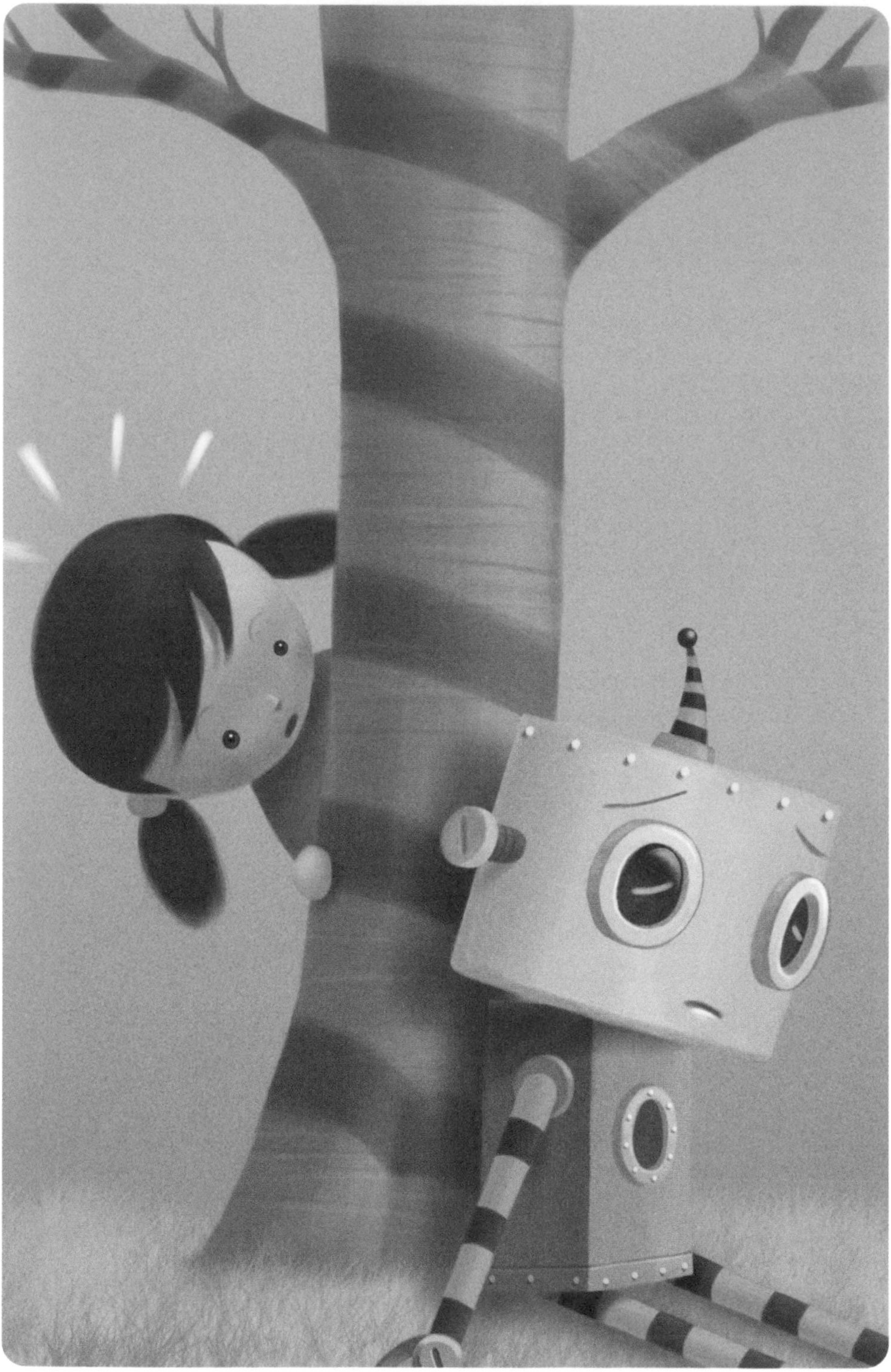

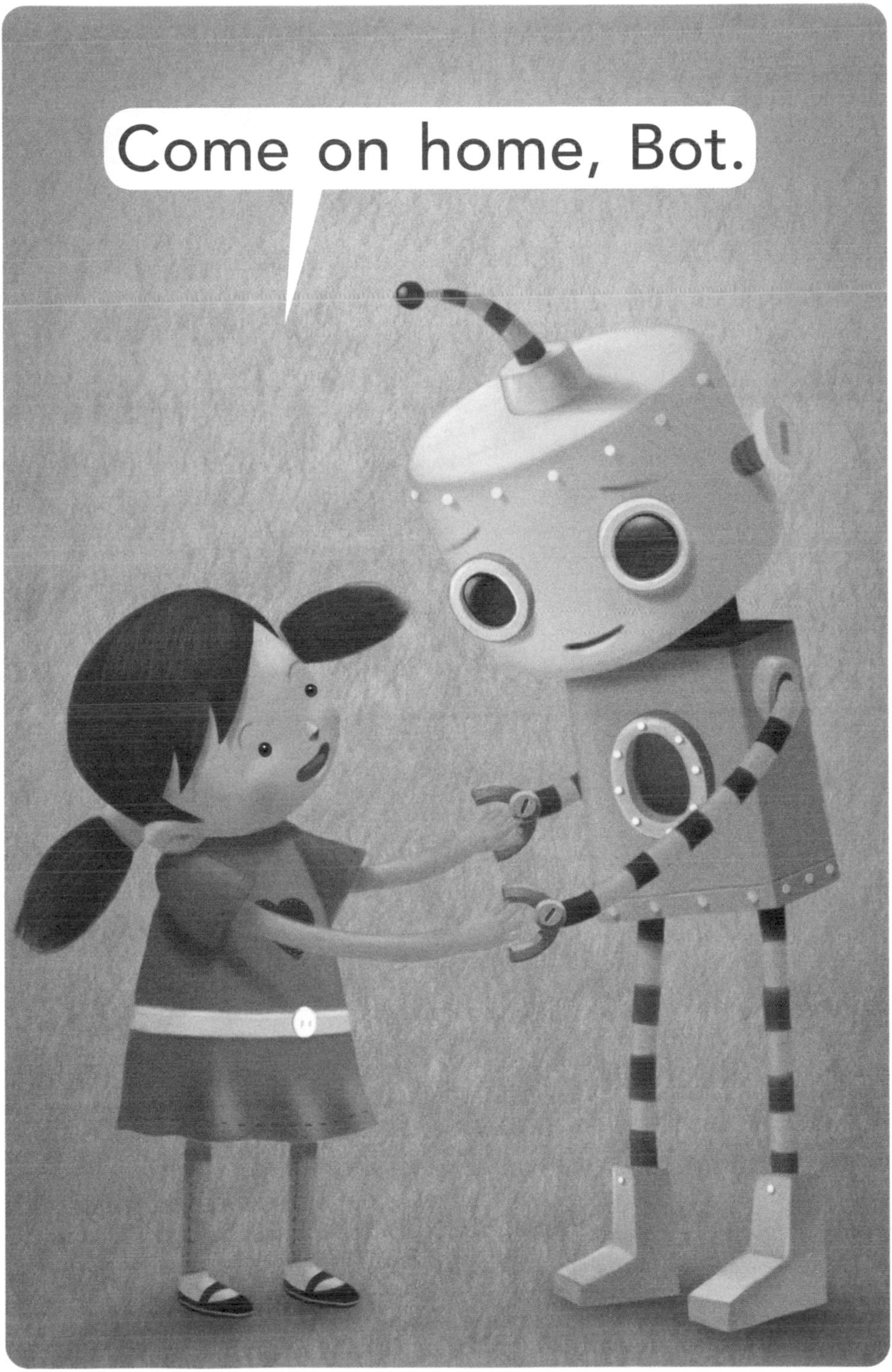
Come on home, Bot.

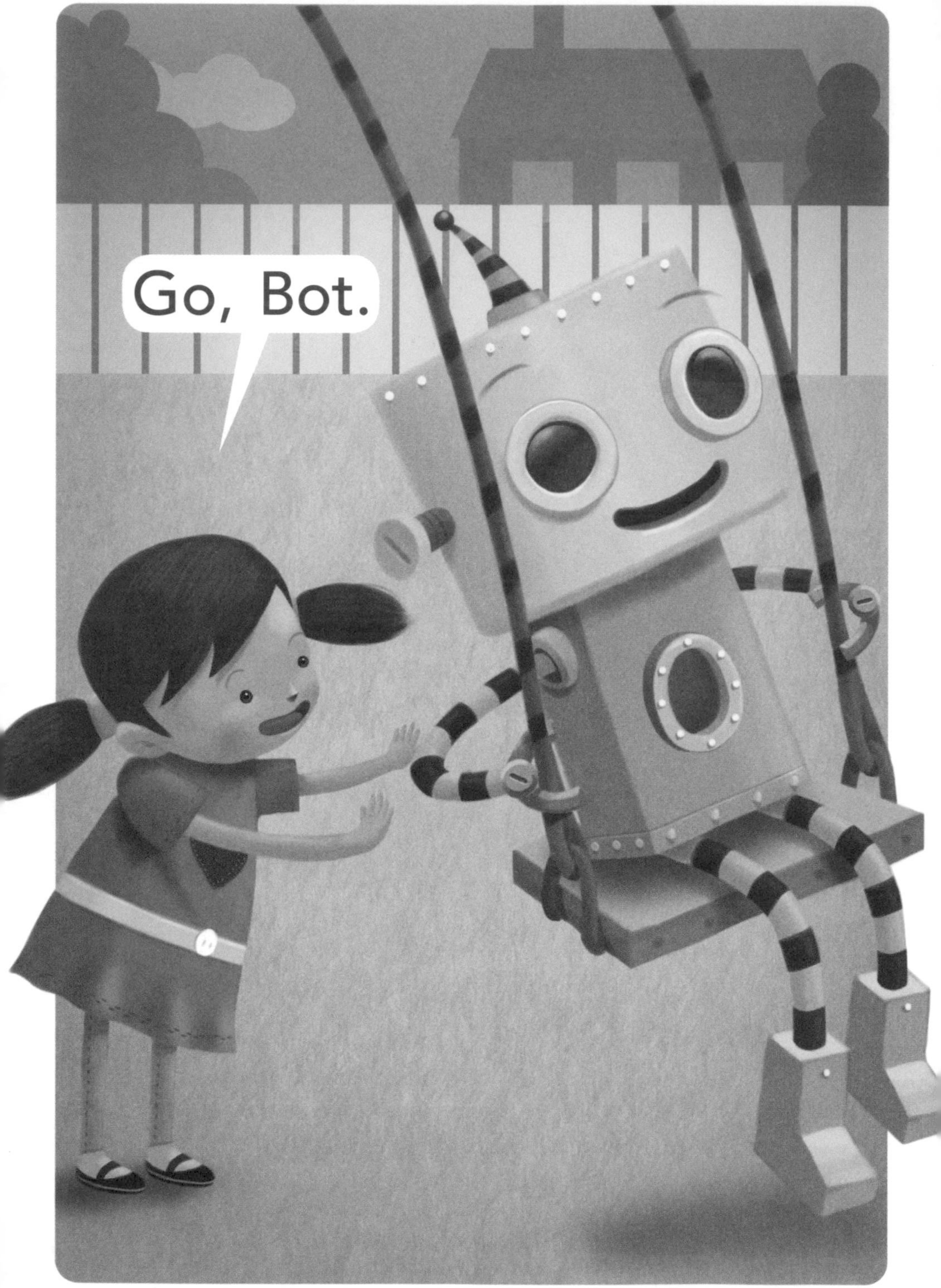
Go, Bot.